PUFFIN BOOKS

The Puffin Book of
Stories for Eight-Year-Olds

Wendy Cooling was educated in Norwich and, after a short time in the Civil Service, spent time travelling the world. On her return to England she trained as a teacher, went on to teach English in London comprehensive schools for many years and was for a time seconded as an advisor on libraries and book-related work in schools. She left teaching to work on the promotion of books and reading as Head of the Children's Book Foundation (now Booktrust), and later founded Bookstart, the national programme that helps to bring books to young readers. She continues to work with the programme as a consultant, as well as working as a freelance book consultant and reviewer.

The Puffin Book of
Stories for

Eight-Year-Olds

Edited by Wendy Cooling

Illustrated by Steve Cox

PUFFIN

PUFFIN BOOKS

Published by the Penguin Group
Penguin Books Ltd, 80 Strand, London WC2R 0RL, England
Penguin Group (USA) Inc., 375 Hudson Street, New York, New York 10014, USA
Penguin Group (Canada), 90 Eglinton Avenue East, Suite 700, Toronto, Ontario, Canada M4P 2Y3
(a division of Pearson Penguin Canada Inc.)
Penguin Ireland, 25 St Stephen's Green, Dublin 2, Ireland (a division of Penguin Books Ltd)
Penguin Group (Australia), 250 Camberwell Road, Camberwell, Victoria 3124, Australia
(a division of Pearson Australia Group Pty Ltd)
Penguin Books India Pvt Ltd, 11 Community Centre, Panchsheel Park, New Delhi – 110 017, India
Penguin Group (NZ), 67 Apollo Drive, Mairangi Bay, Auckland 1310, New Zealand
(a division of Pearson New Zealand Ltd)
Penguin Books (South Africa) (Pty) Ltd, 24 Sturdee Avenue, Rosebank, Johannesburg 2196, South Africa

Penguin Books Ltd, Registered Offices: 80 Strand, London WC2R 0RL, England

penguin.com

First published 1996

036

The Acknowledgements on pages 137–8 constitute an extension of this copyright page

Set in 16/18pt Monophoto Ehrhardt
Made and printed in England by Clays Ltd, St Ives plc

British Library Cataloguing in Publication Data
A CIP catalogue record for this book is available from the British Library

ISBN: 978-0-140-38052-1

www.greenpenguin.co.uk

Contents

Introduction

These stories have all been enjoyed by eight-year-olds and, of course, can be enjoyed by many other children of primary school age. There are stories of real children – children of yesterday, today and tomorrow; myths, legends and fables; stories to wonder at and to appeal to the young imagination. There are stories set in Japan, China, India and Jerusalem; a myth from Greece, along with timeless stories of giants, and more than a touch of magic.

Most eight-year-olds are reading independently but still enjoy that shared experience of listening to a story. These stories are to read aloud at school or at home. The reading can be shared with children who are fluent readers and want to help, but children still lacking in confidence will prefer to listen and may well go back to read the stories alone later. Enjoyment is what is important, because the more positive children feel about stories and reading, the more likely they are to want to look at other books and experience more stories. Remember, story time is not necessarily quiet time – there's much in these tales to discuss and many questions to be answered.

Use this book as a jumping off point. Let it lead you and your children into the rich world of stories old and new, of real life and of magic. Children's imaginations need feeding, they need their heroes, villains, and most of all their dreams. Enjoy these stories and read on!

Wendy Cooling

A Picnic with the Aunts

URSULA MORAY WILLIAMS

There were once six lucky, lucky boys who were invited by their aunts to go on a picnic expedition to an island in the middle of a lake.

The boys' names were Freddie, Adolphus, Edward, Montague, Montmorency and little John Henry. Their aunts were Aunt Bossy, Aunt Millicent, Aunt Celestine, Aunt Miranda, Aunt Adelaide and Auntie Em.

The picnic was to be a great affair, since the lake was ten miles off, and they were to drive there in a wagonette pulled by two grey horses. Once arrived at the lake they were to leave the wagonette and get into a rowing-boat with all the provisions for the picnic, also umbrellas, in case it rained. The aunts were bringing cricket bats, stumps and balls for the boys to play with, and a rope for them to jump over. There was also a box of fireworks to let off at the close of the day when it was getting dark, before they all got into the boat and rowed back to the shore. The wagonette with Davy Driver would leave them at the lake in the morning and come back to fetch them in the evening, at nine o'clock.

The food for the picnic was quite out of this world, for all the aunts were excellent cooks.

There were strawberry tarts, made by Aunt Bossy, and gingerbread covered with almonds baked by Aunt Millicent. Aunt Celestine had prepared a quantity of sausage rolls, while Aunt Miranda's cheese tarts were packed in a tea cosy to keep them warm. Aunt Adelaide had cut so many sandwiches they had to be packed in a suitcase, while Auntie Em had supplied ginger pop, and apples, each one polished like a looking glass on the back of her best serge skirt.

Besides the provisions the aunts had brought their embroidery and their knitting, a book of fairy tales in case the boys were tired, a bottle of physic in case they were ill, and a cane in case they were naughty. And they had invited the boys' headmaster, Mr Hamm, to join the party, as company for themselves and to prevent their nephews from becoming too unruly.

The wagonette called for the boys at nine o'clock in the morning – all the aunts were wearing their best Sunday hats, and the boys had been forced by their mother into their best sailor suits. When Mr Headmaster Hamm had been picked up the party was complete, only he had brought his fiddle with him and the wagonette was really very overcrowded. At each hill the boys were forced to get out and walk, which they considered very unfair, for their headmaster was so fat he must have weighed far more than the six of them put together, but they arrived at the lake at last.

There was a great unpacking of aunts and provisions, a repetition of orders to Davy Driver, and a scolding of little boys, who were running excitedly towards the water's edge with knitting wool wound about their ankles.

A large rowing-boat was moored to a ring on the shore. When it was loaded with passengers and provisions it looked even more overcrowded than the wagonette had done, but Aunt Bossy seized an oar and Mr Headmaster Hamm another – Auntie Em took a third, while two boys manned each of the remaining three.

Amid much splashing and screaming the boat moved slowly away from the shore and inched its way across the lake to the distant island, the boys crashing their oars together while Auntie Em and Aunt Bossy grew pinker and pinker in the face as they strove to keep up with Mr Headmaster Hamm, who rowed in his shirt sleeves, singing the Volga Boat Song.

It was a hot summer's day. The lake lay like a sheet of glass, apart from the long ragged wake behind the boat. Since they all had their backs to the island they hit it long before they realized they had arrived, and the jolt crushed Aunt Millicent's legs between the strawberry tarts and the ginger-beer bottles.

The strawberry jam oozed on to her shins convincing her that she was bleeding to death. She lay back fainting in the arms of Mr Headmaster Hamm, until little John Henry remarked that Aunt Millicent's blood looked just like his favourite jam, whereupon she sat up in a minute, and told him that he was a very disgusting little boy.

Aunt Bossy decided that the boat should be tied up in the shade of some willow trees and the provisions left inside it to keep cool until dinner-time. The boys were very disappointed, for they were all hungry and thought it must be long past dinner-time already.

'You boys can go and play,' Aunt Bossy told them. She gave them the cricket stumps, the bat and ball, and the rope to jump over, but they did not want to jump or play cricket. They wanted to rush about the island and explore, to look for birds' nests and to climb trees, to play at cowboys and Indians and to swim in the lake.

But all the aunts began to make aunt-noises at once:

'Don't get too hot!'

'Don't get too cold!'

'Don't get dirty!'

'Don't get wet!'

'Keep your hats on or you'll get sunstroke!'

'Keep your shoes on or you'll cut your feet!'

'Keep out of the water or you'll be drowned!'

'Don't fight!'

'Don't shout!'

'Be good!'

'Be good!'

'Be good!'

'There! You hear what your aunts say,' added Mr Headmaster Hamm. 'So mind you are good!'

The six aunts and Mr Headmaster Hamm went to sit under the trees to knit and embroider and play the fiddle, leaving the boys standing on the shore, looking gloomily at one another.

'Let's not,' said Adolphus.

'But if we aren't,' said Edward, 'we shan't get any dinner.'

'Let's have dinner first,' suggested little John Henry.

They sat down on the grass above the willow trees looking down on the boat. It was a long time since breakfast and they could not take their eyes off the boxes of provisions tucked underneath the seats, the bottles of ginger pop restored to order, and Auntie Em's basket of shining, rosy apples.

Voices came winging across the island:

'Why are you boys sitting there doing nothing at all? Why can't you find something nice to do on this lovely island?'

Quite coldly and firmly Freddie stood up and faced his brothers.

'Shall we leave them to it?' he suggested.

'What do you mean?' cried Adolphus, Edward, Montague, Montmorency and little John Henry.

'We'll take the boat and the provisions

and row away to the other end of the lake, leaving them behind!' said Freddie calmly.

'Leave them behind on the island!' his brothers echoed faintly.

As the monstrous suggestion sank into their minds all six boys began to picture the fun they might have if they were free of the aunts and of Mr Headmaster Hamm. As if in a dream they followed Freddie to the boat, stepped inside and cast off the rope. At the very last moment Adolphus flung the suitcase of sandwiches ashore before each boy seized an oar and rowed for their lives away from the island.

By the time the six aunts and Mr Headmaster Hamm had realized what was happening the boat was well out into the lake, and the boys took not the slightest notice of the waving handkerchiefs, the calls, the shouts, the pleadings and even the bribes that followed them across the water.

It was a long, hard pull to the end of the lake but not a boy flagged until the bows of the boat touched shore and the island was a blur in the far distance. Then, rubbing the blistered palms of their hands, they jumped ashore, tying the rope to a rock, and tossing the provisions from one to another in a willing chain.

Then began the most unforgettable afternoon of their lives. It started with a feast, when each boy stuffed himself with whatever he fancied most. Ginger-beer bottles popped and fizzed, apple cores were tossed far and wide. When they had finished eating they amused themselves by writing impolite little messages to their aunts and to Mr Headmaster Hamm, stuffing them into the empty bottles and sending them off in the direction of the little island.

They wrote such things as:

'Hey diddle diddle
Old Ham and his fiddle
Sharp at both ends
And flat in the middle!'

'Aunt Miranda has got so thin
She has got nothing to keep her inside in.'

'My Aunt Boss rides a hoss.
Which is boss, hoss or Boss?'

Fortunately, since they forgot to replace the

stoppers, all the bottles went to the bottom long before they reached their goal.

After this they swam in the lake, discovering enough mud and weeds to plaster themselves with dirt until they looked like savages. Drying themselves on the trousers of their sailor suits they dressed again and rushed up into the hills beyond the lake where they discovered a cave, and spent an enchanting afternoon playing at robbers, and hurling great stones down the steep hillside.

Feeling hungry again the boys ate the rest of the provisions, and then, too impatient to wait for the dark, decided to let off the box of fireworks. Even by daylight these provided a splendid exhibition as Freddie lit one after another. Then a spark fell on Montague's collar, burning a large hole, while Montmorency burnt his hand and hopped about crying loudly. To distract him Freddie lit the largest rocket of all, which they had been keeping for the last.

They all waited breathlessly for it to go off, watching the little red spark creep slowly up the twist of paper until it reached the vital spot. With a tremendous hiss the rocket shot into the air. Montmorency stopped sucking his hand and all the boys cheered.

But the rocket hesitated and faltered in mid-flight. It turned a couple of somersaults in the air and dived straight into the boat, landing in the bows with a crash.

Before it could burn the wood or do any damage Freddie rushed after it. With a prodigious bound he leapt into the boat that had drifted a few yards from the shore.

Unfortunately he landed so heavily that his foot went right through one of the boards, and although he seized the stick of the rocket and hurled it far into the lake, the water came through the hole so quickly that the fire would have been quenched in any case.

There was nothing that any of them could do, for the boat was rotten, and the plank had simply given way. They were forced to stand and watch it sink before their eyes in four feet of water.

The sun was setting now. The surrounding hills threw blue shadows into the lake.

A little breeze sprang up ruffling the water. The island seemed infinitely far away.

Soberly, sadly, the six boys began to walk down the shore to the beginning of the lake, not knowing what they would do when they got there. They were exhausted by their long, mad afternoon – some were crying and others limping.

Secretly the younger ones hoped that when they arrived they would find the grown-ups waiting for them, but when they reached the beginning of the lake no grown-ups were there. Not even Davy Driver.

'We will build a fire!' Freddie announced to revive their spirits. 'It will keep us warm and show the aunts we are all safe and well.'

'They get so anxious about us!' said Montmorency.

So they built an enormous bonfire from all the driftwood and dry branches they could find. This cheered them all very much because they were strictly forbidden to make bonfires at home.

It was dark by now, but they had the fire for light, and suddenly the moon rose, full and stately, flooding the lake with a sheet of silver. The boys laughed and shouted. They flung more branches on to the fire and leapt up and down.

Suddenly Adolphus stopped in mid-air and pointed, horror-struck, towards the water.

Far out on the silver lake, sharply outlined against the moonlight, they saw a sight that froze their blood to the marrow.

It was the aunts' hats, drifting towards the shore.

The same little breeze that rippled the water and fanned their fire was blowing the six hats away from the island, and as they floated closer and closer to the shore the boys realized for the first time what a terrible thing they had done, for kind Aunt Bossy, generous Aunt Millicent, good Aunt Celestine, devoted Aunt Miranda, worthy Aunt Adelaide and dear *dear* Auntie Em, together with their much respected headmaster, Mr Hamm, had all been DROWNED!

Freddie, Adolphus, Edward, Montague, Montmorency and little John Henry burst into tears of such genuine repentance and grief that it would have done their aunts good to hear them. They sobbed so bitterly that after a while they had no more tears left to weep, and it was little John Henry who first wiped his eyes on his sleeve and recovered his composure. The next moment his mouth opened wide and his eyes seemed about to burst out of his head.

He pointed a trembling finger towards the lake and all his brothers looked where he was pointing. Then their eyes bulged too and their mouths dropped open as they beheld the most extraordinary sight they had ever dreamed of.

The aunts were swimming home!

For under the hats there were heads, and behind the heads small wakes of foam bore witness to the efforts of the swimmers.

The hats were perfectly distinguishable. First came Aunt Bossy's blue hydrangeas topped by a purple bow, then Aunt Millicent's little lilac bonnet. Close behind Aunt Millicent came Aunt Celestine's boater, smartly ribboned in green plush, followed by Aunt Miranda's black velvet toque, with a bunch of violets. Then some

metres further from the shore a floral plat-
ter of pansies and roses that Aunt Adelaide
had bought to open a Church Bazaar. And
last of all came Auntie Em in her pink straw
pillbox hat, dragging behind her with a rope
the picnic suitcase, on which was seated Mr
Headmaster Hamm, who could not swim.

Holding the sides of the suitcase very
firmly with both hands, he carried between
his teeth, as a dog carries a most important
bone, the aunts' cane.

Motionless and petrified, with terror
and relief boiling together in their veins,
Freddie, Adolphus, Edward, Montague,
Montmorency and little John Henry stood
on the shore – the fire shining on their filthy
suits, dirty faces and sodden shoes, while
slowly, steadily, the aunts swam back from
the island, and far behind them over the
hills appeared at last the lights of Davy
Driver's wagonette, coming to fetch them
home.

The Story of the Small Boy and the Barley-Sugar

MAX BEERBOHM

Little reader, unroll your map of England.

Look over its coloured counties and find
Rutland.

You shall not read this story till you have
found Rutland; for it was
there, and in the village of Dauble, that
these things happened.

You need not look for Dauble; it is too small
to be marked.

*

There was only one shop in the village, and it was kept by Miss Good, and every one was very proud of it.

A little further down the street there was, indeed, a black, noisy place with flames in it. This was kept by a frightening man, who wore a great beard, and did not go to the church on Sundays. But I do not think it was a real shop, for only the horses went there. The children always ran past it very quickly.

The children never ran past Miss Good's, unless they were late for school. They used to crowd round the window and talk about the red and yellow sweets, which were banked up against the glass in a most tempting and delightful fashion. Sometimes one of the boys, more greedy than the rest, would stand on tiptoe and press his lips to the glass, declaring he could nearly taste the sweets, or 'lollypops', as he called them. Sometimes Miss Good would come and nod her ringlets to the children, over the bottles of homemade peppermint. How they envied her, living always, as she did, in company so sweet and splendid!

They were not rich, these little children. But most of them were good, and often, when they had been very good, their parents would give them brown pennies. Hardly a day passed but one of them would strut forth from the rest and go solemnly into the shop, soon to return with treasure wrapped in paper. This happy child – were it boy or girl – seldom broke the rather harsh law that compelled the bag to be handed round among the other children, first. His or hers were all the sweets that remained. Therefore pear-drops were usually chosen, because they were so small, and half an ounce meant very many pear-drops.

Out of school-hours, Miss Good's window was seldom free from its wistful crowd. Indeed, a certain small boy, named Tommy Tune, was the only one of all the schoolchildren who did not seem to love it. Was he not fond of sweets? He was indeed. Was he never good enough to be given a penny? He was almost always good. But, alas! his parents were so poor that they had no pennies to spare for him. When first he went to the school he used to go and look at the sweet shop with the other boys and girls, and always took a sweet when it was offered him. But soon he grew ashamed of taking sweets, he, who was never able to give any in return. And so he kept away. If he were ever to have a penny, he was going to buy a stick of barley-sugar and share it with Jill Trellis. She was eight years old, like him, and she had curly brown hair and blue eyes, and he loved her. But she was unkind to him, because he never had a penny. She would not go and play with him in the fields, as he asked her, but preferred to be with the other boys. When Tommy saw her in the distance eating their sweets or running races with them, or playing at kiss-in-the-ring with them, his cheeks grew very red, and his eyes filled with tears. But somehow he loved her all the more. And he often used to dream of Jill, and of pennies, and of the window that Jill loved.

There were other things than sweets in this window, but they were seldom sold. There were strips of bacon, which were not wanted, because every cottager had a pig. There were bright ribbons round reels, but the girls of that village were not vain, and fairs were few. From the low ceiling hung bunches of tallow-candles, seeming to grow there like fruit, but every one in that village went to bed at sunset. There was starch, but why stiffen linen? And bootlaces, but they always break.

So Miss Good, like a sensible person, had devoted herself to the study of sweets, how to make them cheaply and well, and, as she was fond of little children, she was pleased that they were her chief customers. But it so happened that she herself was also very fond of sweets. She enjoyed tasting them, not only when she wished to see if they were good, but also when she knew quite well that they were good.

Now, one summer's evening, when all the children had gone home to bed and she was putting up her humble shutters, Miss Good remembered suddenly that it was her birth-day. You see, she had not had one for a whole year, and had forgotten that there were such things. She smiled to herself as she bolted the door of her shop, murmuring softly:

'I must really celebrate my birthday!'

So she cut down one of the tallow-candles and, having lit it, set it upon the counter.

'Illuminations!' she murmured.

Then she cast her eye slowly over all the variegated sweets that were in the window. With deft fingers she selected some of every kind, piling them all, at length, upon the counter. In the fair light of the candle they sparkled like precious stones.

I am sorry to say that the next morning, when Miss Good awoke, she felt very ill, and regretted, not only that it had been her birthday, but she had ever been born at all. She felt that she could not serve in the shop that day. And this was serious, for she had no assistant and thus might lose much custom.

Miss Good was at all times, however, a woman of resource. Rising from her bed, she threw open the little lattice window and called softly for the Queen of the Fairies, with whom, by the way, she was distantly connected. Then she returned to her bed.

In less than a minute, the convolvulus-chariot and team of dragon-flies flew in at the window, and drew up sharp at the foot of the bed. Dismissing with a word her escort of butterflies, the tiny Queen alighted on the counterpane, and said:

'Miss Good, why did you call for Us?'

The invalid confessed how greedy she had been, and implored the Queen not to think ill of her. And Her Majesty, knowing well that the sellers of sweets must ever be exposed to stronger temptations than are ordinary folk, smiled upon her not unkindly.

'Could you possibly,' murmured Miss Good from her pillow, 'without inconvenience, send a fairy to mind the shop, just for today?'

'On the condition that you never again exceed,' said the Queen.

'I promise,' said Miss Good. 'Thank you very much. My head aches sadly. I am best alone. Thanks. Remember me kindly to the King.'

With a gracious inclination of her head, Her Majesty stepped into her chariot and was gone.

Now, as it happened, Tommy Tune's father came home that morning from another village, where for some days he had been making hay. The kind farmer, whose hay it was, had paid him very handsomely for his work. And when Tommy, having eaten his dinner, took his slate and was starting again for school, his father called him back.

'Tommy, son,' he said, 'I've brought back something for you. Shut your eyes and give me your hand.'

Tommy obeyed in wonder. When he opened his eyes and looked to see what was in his hand, he saw – what do you think? – a real, brown penny!

'Oh father,' he cried, 'how wonderful it is! And can you really spare it?'

'I'm not sure that I can,' replied Mr Tune, rather grimly. 'Run away now before I ask for it back.'

And Tommy scampered off.

Far down the road, on the way to school, walked a little girl, whose brown hair curled over her pinafore. It was Jill. He shouted to her to stop, and ran still faster. Yesterday he would not have dared to speak to her, certainly not to shout.

When he came nearer, the little girl heard him and looked round. At first she shook her head and began walking on, but Tommy called to her so eagerly that at length she waited for him.

'Jill!' he said to her, shy and breathless, 'will you come with me after school and buy barley-sugar?'

'No, I won't,' she said. 'I'm going to play at horses with Dicky Jones. And what's more, I haven't a penny. And if I had I shouldn't go with you, because I don't like you.'

'But *I* have a penny, Jill,' he pleaded.

'Show it!' rejoined the little girl.

Tommy showed it.

'Well,' she said, after a while, 'I won't play at horses today. And I – I think you're much nicer than Dicky Jones. And – and – oh, Tommy! why are you always so unkind to me now?'

When they came to the school, the school-bell had almost ceased tolling, and all the children had gone in. Just outside the porch, Jill whispered:

'Tommy, I'm not angry with you. Kiss me. Quickly!'

And in another moment, they went in too.

How very slowly the time went for Tommy that afternoon! He could only just see the top of Jill's curly head. She always sat far away from him, for, though she was a girl, she was cleverer than he was, and was in a higher class. But he thought about her all the time. The big round figures seemed to write themselves on his slate, he knew not how. Whenever a 'nought' came, he put four little dots in it; two for Jill's eyes, one for her nose, one for her mouth. And all his sums came out right that afternoon, long before the other boys and girls had done theirs. Then there was nothing for him to do, but to keep his eyes on the clock. Thirty whole minutes more! What was thirty times sixty?

He remembered that Jill's class did its spelling lesson in the last half-hour. Jill would stand up with the rest by the teacher's desk. Perhaps she would look round at him. He could scarcely believe that soon they would be sitting together, all alone in the field, with a stick of barley-sugar.

When Jill went up with the others to the high desk, she did look round at Tommy, with her finger to her lips, just where he had kissed her. In another instant she had clasped her hands behind her and was looking up at the teacher.

She was near the top of her class, and her turn came soon. She was given a very easy word to spell; but she must have been thinking of other things, I am afraid, for she missed it. She spelt *Cow* with a *U*. Tommy, in his corner, blushed scarlet.

When her turn came round again, she spelt *Kite* with a *C*. The teacher, who had always thought her to be one of the best of her pupils, frowned.

'Be careful, Jill Trellis!' she said sharply.

Tommy held his slate very tightly with both hands.

Then Jill was told to spell *Box*.

'*B*,' she said, '*O*.' Then she stopped short. Then she shook her head.

'Be very careful,' said the teacher. 'You cannot be attending. *B*, *O* – well?'

Jill shook her head.

'*X*,' said the teacher. 'Abominable little girl! Fetch the Dunce's cap and stand on the stool. You will stay here for an hour after school is over and learn two pages of hard words.'

So Jill fetched the Dunce's cap and climbed up on to the stool and clasped her hands behind her.

Nor did she look at Tommy when the clock struck four, and the schoolchildren trooped out.

For some time Tommy stood in the porch. There, at least, he was near his poor sweetheart. He would wait there till she was set free.

But somehow, as the minutes went by, he grew more and more miserable. He could not bear to think of her in there with her spelling-book. He would run away somewhere and be at the gate to meet her when she came out.

As he ran, it struck him that she might be comforted if he met her with the barley-sugar in his hand. And so he stopped at the door of Miss Good's shop and walked boldly in.

To his surprise, Miss Good, whose ringlets he had often seen through the window, was not there, and in her stead, smiling from behind the counter, was a beautiful young person with bright yellow hair and blue wings.

'Good afternoon, little sir,' said the young person, 'what may I serve you with?'

'A penny stick of barley-sugar,' said Tommy. He spoke in rather a surly voice, for he did not like any one to be pretty except Jill; though Jill, of course, was far prettier than this stranger, in his opinion.

'What a pleasant afternoon, is it not?' said the young person, taking from a glass bottle a short, twisted stick of barley-sugar.

Tommy stretched out his hand in silence.

'Quite seasonable!' she continued, looking down at her little customer and holding the stick just beyond his reach. 'But you are behaving as if it were mid-winter and the snow had smothered the flowers. I suppose you are what would be called unhappy.'

'Yes, I am,' said Tommy sulkily, 'and I want the barley-sugar.'

'Certainly, little sir,' replied the young person. 'I will not detain you.' Lightly she blew upon the yellow stick. 'Now, understand,' she said, 'that every time you take a bit at that, you can wish, and all your wishes will come true. Say "thank you", and give me your penny.'

Tommy opened his eyes very wide and thanked her.

'Good afternoon,' she said, dropping his penny into the till.

Tommy ran, as hard as he could, to a certain field. He held the barley-sugar tightly in his hand. He knew what he was going to wish for first. His eyes sparkled as he ran. Visions of what he would wish for later on came vaguely to his mind – a lovely garden of roses for his mother, a lovely farm for his father, for himself a regiment of wooden soldiers, taller than he was. But these fair visions he hardly heeded. He was thinking only of his first wish.

That he might get more quickly into the field, he climbed through a break in the hedge, caring not how the brambles scratched him, and jumped over the ditch on to the grass beyond. He stood there, after his run, flushed and trembling with excitement. He put the sweet yellow stick to his lips and set his teeth upon the very edge of it, so as not to take more than a tiny bite. Then, shutting his eyes tight, he said aloud:

'I wish that Jill may come here at once.'

And, when he looked, there stood Jill before him, in her Dunce's cap. There was a spelling-book in her hand, and her eyes were full of tears. But Tommy flung his arms round her neck so quickly that the book and the cap both fell to the ground. Tommy kissed away all her tears.

'Leave go, Tommy!' she cried at last. 'Tell me why I am here? I was in the school-room. Why am I in this field?'

'I wished for you to come to me, Jill,' the boy answered.

'But I was in the schoolroom!' said Jill.

'This is a stick of barley-sugar,' Tommy began.

'So it is,' said Jill, drawing nearer. 'It looks good.'

'But it isn't like the others,' Tommy went on, 'because you see, a fairy gave it me for my penny, and when you take a bite you wish, and your wish comes true. I wished for you, Jill. And I'm going to wish for – oh! heaps of things. You shall wish too.'

'May I?' cried Jill.

Swiftly she snatched the yellow stick from his hand and ran away, crushing it all into her mouth at once.

'Jill! Jill!' cried the boy piteously, as he chased her round the field. 'Do leave a little!'

At length he caught her and held her fast in his arms. 'Haven't you left a little?' he asked her.

She shook her head from side to side. Her mouth was too full for speech.

'And, Jill! you never wished!' he said sadly.

'Oh yes, I did,' she answered presently. 'I wished that you hadn't eaten that first bit.'

Little reader, roll up your map of England.

But first look once more at Rutland, that you may remember where it is.

Perhaps you have often laughed at Rutland, because it is the tiniest of all the counties, and is painted pink.

Now see how neatly and well they have painted it, never going over the edges, as you would have done.

And know, also, that though it looks so small, it is really more than three times as big as your nursery, and that things can happen there.

It is very foolish to laugh at Rutland.

The Girl Who Stayed for Half a Week

GENE KEMP

Nobody much noticed her come. Except for me and Miss. Nobody much noticed her go. Except for Miss and me. And that wasn't because of *her* but because I always noticed Miss. I liked to watch her. She reminded me of something – someone – somewhere, I couldn't quite remember, like the dream that slithers away out of reach when you wake in the morning and no matter how you try to bring it back it vanishes for good. Not

33

that Miss was going to disappear, var-romph, gone (I hope). Or like that feeling that pulls you round the next corner just to see what's beyond, or run to the top of the hill when you can hardly get your breath because there might, there just possibly might be something fabulous, fantastic, amazing, strange, wonderful, waiting there, just out of sight, on the other side. That was just the feeling Miss gave me.

Some kids hate their teacher. I nearly hated Mrs Baker last year. She always put me down. Look where you're putting your feet, Michael, must your work be so untidy, so messy, Michael, do you have to take up so much room, Michael? I couldn't help being me and sprouting in all directions. I couldn't help growing. I didn't tell myself to grow. I just did. But in the end I didn't hate her, there being other things to think about. In fact I gave her a box of chocolates at the end of the year, though I didn't choose my favourites and five other kids gave her the same kind.

But Miss is something else. If Miss reads something you've written and she thinks it's good she smiles at the pages before she says anything as if she understands the meaning behind the words you wrote on the page, sad or frightening or funny. She's got grey eyes and curly brown hair and a curly grin with a crooked tooth and she's not very big so I reach things down from the shelves for her, being the tallest in the class though Greg Grubber is wider. Maybe that's because my Dad's gynormous and feeds me on super grub (he's a great cook) or because he made me go to aikido classes and I'm a blue belt now. 'It'll help to stop you putting your great big hoofs everywhere and smashing everything,' he said. That was after Mum died, and I didn't know whether I was crashing and smashing everywhere because of my feet or because there was just a big black hole that I kept falling into no matter what I did. But that's not what this story's about . . .

It's about a girl who came and went and changed my life without knowing. I don't suppose I'll ever see her again to thank her, or even say hello. She came into our

classroom in the middle of a Monday afternoon. I'd just looked up from the project I
was doing (on oil) and there she stood
by Miss's desk, a kind of smudge of a girl
like a crayon drawing that Grubber might
walk past and rub into rubbish with his
elbow if he felt in the mood for a spot of
aggro.

This girl looked as if someone had made
quite a good job of her in the first place and
then some toe-rag such as Grubber had
rubbed her over, leaving her little and tired
and pale and a bit dirty with a light turned
off somewhere. Everyone in the room
seemed busy – the projects were to be
handed in by Tuesday – so I was the only
one watching as Miss talked to her, because
I'd looked up to see if Miss was OK.

You're saying, are you out of your tiny
deformed mind, then? You might be big in
the body but you've obviously got a brain
the size of a pea. Look, idiot face, your
teacher's supposed to *look after you*, not the
other way round, OK. And yeah, we know
you lost your mum, sorry, that was bad, but
does it have to mean you have to mooch

round after your teachers like a camel with a toothache?

I know all that, me, Michael Haines, I know all about it. So you can just leave the preaching and accept that I raised my eyes and saw this deprived-looking kid drooping by Miss's desk as if she'd rather be any- where else at all in the whole world, even if it meant being dead or something. Miss was smiling at her as she does and I know she'd be asking her name, and how old, and did she like reading and so on. I've heard her with other new kids. She was welcoming, smiling at her as if she was wonderful, all smudgy as she was – the kid, not Miss.

So I decided I'd wander up to that desk to borrow the stapler. Not that I needed the stapler just then but it made a good excuse. We've only got one in the classroom and you have to ask for it ever since Grubber tried to staple one of the mice from the En- vironment Area to a piece of card. When I got to the desk I heard Miss say, 'You needn't read to me this afternoon if you're tired.' And this girl, who just about came up to my knees, making me wonder what she was doing in our class (one of four top-year ones) gazed into Miss's face, then put down her head so her tatty hair fell everywhere, climbed on to Miss's knee, stuck her thumb in her mouth and her head on Miss's shoulder.

Now I knew I'd got to conceal this awful sight from some of our class members – Grubber not being the only one with a Heavy Metal inside – so I positioned myself between them and the class. Then Miss put her gently down, but still holding her hand, stood up and told all of us to put our things away.

'We'll have a story and a poem for the end of the afternoon,' she said.

So we did. She read to us about a boy who went into a garden at midnight and what he found there. We sat and listened, even Grubber. He enjoys stories more than he admits.

'Anything's better than work, dog's breath,' he says.

The girl hadn't yet got a seat to sit down on. She stood by Miss, holding her baggy sweater as if she might fly straight off

Planet Earth if she let go, or sink down beneath the school, through the foundations and the rocks below, right down to the fiery centre of the planet. After a few minutes she climbed back on to Miss's knee, stuck her thumb in her mouth and her head on Miss's shoulder and this time stayed there as if she'd arrived home and wasn't leaving it, ever. Funnily enough, no one took any notice, as if they were just too lost in the story and she was part of it.

Next day she came late and was given her desk and books and so on. Later Miss heard her read and checked her maths and writing etc at her desk. And as we did our work she stayed there as if she never wanted to leave that place. At playtime I got ready to flatten Grubber if he started any of his funnies but there was no need. She stayed in. So did Miss, and anyone else who wished.

At the end of the afternoon, after clearing up, Miss brought out the story. The girl climbed on to her lap and held her as before.

*

On the fourth day Grubber at last registered she was there and went up to where she was doing her work at the side of Miss's desk. Miss was with a group in the far corner of the room.

'What's all this, then?' asked Grubber, in a voice like a Rottweiler with laryngitis. 'How you come gits doin' your rubbish 'ere. You ain't no special right 'ere. Git lost, vomit.'

Now Grubber and me, we've always scrapped. Yes, all the way up from toddler group, playgroup, Infants and through to the Middle. We fought at two, three, four, five, six, seven, eight, then at nine I started to go to aikido. After that he couldn't win any more though that didn't stop him trying. No style, though, no discipline, only size and power. Yeah, Grubber's got that. Power.

And he intended using it. He meant to turf out little Smudge from her safe place by Miss's chair. He fancied doing that. Not that he wanted to be there himself, oh no, the further he was from any teacher the better, but if this new kid wanted to be there that wouldn't do. Grubber couldn't have that. He got ready to move her.

But I was there first.

'She can work here if she wants to.'

'What's with you, snail slime?'

We were both shouting in whispers now . . .

'Leave her alone.'

'Get lost, sewer.'

. . . in case Miss heard. If she hadn't been in the room there would've been a scrap but –

The sound of feet running down the corridor outside.

A scream.

Another scream. 'Stop him!'

A bell. A buzzer. 'Ring the police!'

More running feet.

More screams. Louder now. And louder.

The door burst open. Miss stood up and came out of her corner.

The woman who'd rushed in, white, scared, looked round, ran to little Smudge by the desk, grabbed her and raced *behind* Miss.

'Save me! Save me!' she was babbling.

A man burst in, as red as she was white, big, angry, bald, shirtsleeves flapping.

Miss held out her arms.

'Stop!' she cried.

He went to shove her aside.

'I'm going to get you. You're coming home with me,' he shouted, and pushed Miss away. She crashed into a desk.

My stomach did a freefall.

So among the shouts, the screams, the bangs, I looked at Grubber and Grubber nodded back. Like friends for ever and always we moved in. Grubber chopped him in the back. I high-kicked him just where it hurts.

He went down and we sat on him. So did half the class as into the room poured the school secretary, the head teacher, several helpers and most of the other fourth years.

The head teacher hauled the man to his feet. He looked a bit shattered, as well he might. There seemed to be hundreds of people in our classroom as the police arrived. And then the woman threw her arms round him and he put his arms round her. They were both crying. In the confusion I think only two people noticed little Smudge slip out of the room. Me and Miss. Miss called out and I tried to follow but there were too many people and too much noise.

The next day was Friday. At the end of it Miss went on with *Tom's Midnight Garden*. We sat quiet and subdued. The girl hadn't appeared. At the end of the afternoon I went up to Miss where she sat looking as sad as she had that time Julie Trent had asked why she wasn't wearing her pretty ring any more. Things didn't work out, that's why, Julie, she'd said, things don't always work out.

'Why didn't that girl come?' I asked.

'Oh, she won't be coming here any more. She was staying at the Refuge, but they've all gone back home now. A good thing, I expect. I hope.' She didn't sound at all sure.

'You liked her a lot, didn't you, Miss?'

'Yes, I did. Well, it's Friday, Michael, and time to go.'

My father stood at the door. He hadn't been into school so far this term because of his

43

working hours. He strode towards Miss.

'I had to come to see you,' he said to her, 'to see what really happened yesterday. I heard a most extraordinary story from Michael. I haven't seen him so upset for ages.'

She told him, but it seemed to me that what they were really doing was looking at each other as if they'd just seen a miracle, and what they were saying wasn't all that important.

Somebody nudged me.

'You comin', then? Thought you might like to try out me new bike.'

It was Grubber. We ran out together.

Oh yeah, they got married, my dad and Miss, some time later, when I'd gone to my next school with my mate Grubber.

As a mum she's not the dream round the corner or the something fantastic on the other side of the hill, but she's OK. She'll do. Sometimes she gets a funny look though, and I get this odd feeling that she's remembering the girl who only stayed for half a week and looked as if she'd been smudged.

King Midas – A Greek Myth

GERALDINE McCAUGHREAN

There was once a king called Midas who was almost as stupid as he was greedy.

When there was a music competition between the two gods Pan and Apollo, Midas was asked to be judge. Now Pan was Midas' friend, so instead of listening to the music to judge whose was best, he decided to let Pan win even before they began to play.

Comparing Apollo's music with Pan's is like comparing a golden trumpet with a tin whistle. But Midas had already made up his mind.

'Pan was the better! Oh definitely! No doubt about it. Pan was the better,' he said. On and on he went, praising Pan, until Apollo turned quite scarlet with rage and pointed a magic finger at King Midas.

'There is something wrong with your ears if you think Pan's music is better than mine.'

'Nothing's wrong with my ears,' said foolish King Midas.

'Oh no? Well, we can soon change that!'

When he got home, Midas' ears were itching. He looked in the mirror and – horror of horrors! – his ears were growing. Longer and long they grew, furrier and furrier, until he had brown and pink donkey's ears.

Midas found he could hide the ears if he crammed them both into a tall hat. 'Nobody must see them,' he thought as he walked about with his hat pulled down over his eyes. All day he wore it. He even wore it at night, so that the queen would not see his ass's ears.

Nobody noticed. It was a great relief. They only saw that the king wore a tall hat all day long, and hurried to do the same, thinking it was the latest fashion.

But there was one person from whom Midas could not hide his secret. When the barber came to cut his hair, the dreadful truth came out.

The barber gasped. The barber stared. The barber stuffed a towel into his mouth to keep himself from laughing.

'You will tell no one!' commanded King Midas.

'Of course not! Never! No one! I promise!' babbled the barber, and cut the king's hair and helped him back on with his hat. It was to be their secret, never to be told.

The barber had given his promise. He never broke his promises. But oh dear! It was such a hard secret to keep! He ached to tell somebody. He would suddenly burst out laughing in public and could not explain why. He lay awake at nights, for fear of talking in his sleep. He kept that secret until he thought it would burn holes in him! But at last he just had to tell it.

The barber took a very long walk, right

away from town, all the way to the river. He dug a hole in the ground and put his head deep down it. Then he whispered into the hole, '*King Midas has long ass's ears!*'

After that, he felt a lot better.

And the rain rained and the grass grew and the reeds by the river grew too.

Meanwhile, Midas (wearing his tall cap, of course) was walking in his garden when he met a satyr – half-man, half-horse. The satyr was lost. Midas gave him breakfast and directed him on his way.

'I'm so grateful,' said the satyr. 'Permit me to reward you. I shall grant you one wish.'

He could have wished to be rid of his ass's ears, but no. At once Midas' head filled with pictures of money, wealth, treasure . . . *gold*! His eyes glistened. 'Oh please, please! Grant that everything I touch turns to gold!'

'Oof. Not a good idea,' said the satyr. 'Think again.'

But Midas insisted. That was his wish. The satyr shrugged and went on his way.

'Huh! I knew it was too good to be true,' said King Midas and he was so disappointed that he picked up a pebble to throw after the satyr.

The stone turned to gold in his palm.

'My wish! The satyr granted it after all!' cried Midas, and did a little dance on the spot. He ran to a tree and touched it. Sure enough, the twigs and branches turned to gold. He ran back to his palace and stroked every wall, chair, table and lamp. They all turned to gold. When he brushed against the curtains, even they turned solid with a sudden clang.

'Prepare me a feast!' Midas commanded. 'Being rich makes me hungry!'

The servants ran to fetch meat and bread, fruit and wine, while Midas touched each dish and plate (because it pleased him to eat off gold). When the food arrived, he clutched up a wing of chicken and bit into it.

Clang. It was hard and cold between his lips. The celery scratched his tongue. The bread broke a tooth. Every bite of food turned to gold as he touched it. The wine rattled in its goblet, solid as an egg in an egg cup.

'Don't stand there staring! Fetch me something I can eat!' Midas told a servant, giving him a push . . . But it was a golden statue of a servant that toppled over and fell with a thud.

Just then, the queen came in. 'What's this I hear about a wish?' she asked, and went to kiss her husband.

'Don't come near! Don't touch me!' he shrieked, and jumped away from her. But his little son, who was too young to understand, ran and hugged Midas around the knees. 'Papa! Papa! Pa –'

Silence. His son was silent. The boy's golden arms were still hooped round Midas' knees. His little golden mouth was open, but no sound came out.

Midas ran to his bedroom and locked the door. But he could not sleep that night, for the pillow turned to gold under his head. He was so hungry, so thirsty, so lonely. So afraid. 'Oh you gods! Take away this dreadful wish! I never realized!'

There was a clip-clopping of hoofs and

the satyr put his head through the window. 'I did try to tell you,' he said.

Midas fell on his knees on the golden floor. His golden robe clanged and swung on him like a giant bell. His tall cap fell to the ground like a metal cooking pot. 'Take it back! Please ask the gods to take back my wish!' he begged.

'With ears like that, I think you have troubles enough,' said the satyr, laughing loudly. 'Very well. Go and wash in the river. But do remember not to be so silly another time.'

King Midas ran through the long grass, pushed his way through the long reeds, and leapt into the river. The ripples filled with gold dust, but the water itself did not turn to gold. Nor did the river bank as Midas pulled himself out. He was cured!

He carried buckets of water back to the palace and threw them over the little golden statue in the dining room. And there stood his little son, soaked from head to foot and starting to cry.

By this time, the grass had grown tall in the

fields, and the reeds by the river were taller still. When the wind blew they rustled. When the wind blew harder they murmured. When the wind blew harder still they whispered, '*King Midas has long ass's ears!*'

And on some windy days the reeds sang so loudly that everyone heard them for miles around: '*King Midas has long ass's ears!*'

And that is how King Midas' secret is known to us all today.

A Fish of the World

TERRY JONES

A herring once decided to swim right round the world. 'I'm tired of the North Sea,' he said. 'I want to find out what else there is in the world.'

So he swam off south into the deep Atlantic. He swam and swam far far away from the seas he knew, through the warm waters of the equator and on down into the South Atlantic. And all the time he saw many strange and wonderful fish that he had never seen before. Once he was nearly eaten by a shark, and once he was nearly electrocuted by an electric eel, and once he was nearly stung by a sting-ray. But he swam on and on, round the tip of Africa and into the Indian Ocean. And he passed by devilfish and sailfish and sawfish and swordfish and bluefish and blackfish and mudfish and sunfish, and he was amazed by the different shapes and sizes and colours.

On he swam, into the Java Sea, and he saw fish that leapt out of the water and fish that lived on the bottom of the sea and fish that could walk on their fins. And on he swam, through the Coral Sea, where the shells of millions and millions of tiny creatures had turned to rock and stood as big as mountains. But still he swam on, into the wide Pacific. He swam over the deepest parts of the ocean, where the water is so deep that it is inky black at the bottom, and the fish carry lanterns over their heads, and some have lights on their tails. And through the Pacific he swam, and then he turned north and headed up to the cold Siberian Sea, where huge white icebergs sailed past him like mighty ships. And still he swam on and on and into the frozen Arctic Ocean, where the sea is for ever covered in ice. And on he went, past Greenland and Iceland, and finally he swam home into his own North Sea.

All his friends and relations gathered round and made a great fuss of him. They had a big feast and offered him the very best food they could find. But the herring just yawned and said: 'I've swum round the entire world. I have seen everything there is to see, and I have eaten more exotic and wonderful dishes than you could possibly imagine.' And he refused to eat anything.

Then his friends and relations begged him to come home and live with them, but he refused. 'I've been everywhere there is, and that old rock is too dull and small for me.' And he went off and lived on his own.

And when the breeding season came, he refused to join in the spawning, saying: 'I've swum around the entire world, and now I know how many fish there are in the world, I can't be interested in herrings anymore.'

Eventually, one of the oldest of the herrings swam up to him, and said: 'Listen. If you don't spawn with us, some herrings' eggs will go unfertilized and will not turn into healthy young herrings. If you don't live with your family, you'll make them sad. And if you don't eat, you'll die.'

But the herring said: 'I don't mind. I've been everywhere there is to go, I've seen everything there is to see, and now I know everything there is to know.'

The old fish shook his head. 'No one has ever seen everything there is to see,' he said, 'nor known everything there is to know.'

'Look,' said the herring, 'I've swum through the North Sea, the Atlantic Ocean, the Indian Ocean, the Java Sea, the Coral Sea, the great Pacific Ocean, the Siberian Sea and the frozen Arctic. Tell me, what else is there for me to see or know?'

'I don't know,' said the old herring, 'but there may be something.'

Well, just then, a fishing-boat came by, and all the herrings were caught in a net and taken to market that very day. And a man bought the herring, and ate it for his supper.

And he never knew that it had swum right round the world, and had seen everything there was to see, and knew everything there was to know.

Dog, Cat and Monkey

MICHAEL ROSEN

Dog and Cat are fighting over some meat. Dog's got his jaws round the bone, Cat's got his claws into the flesh. They heave and they tug, but the moment Dog thinks he's got it, Cat gives it a tug. Then the moment Cat thinks he's got it, Dog gets his teeth round a bit more. Neither of them is winning.

Monkey comes to have a look.

Soon he's dancing around giving advice: 'Go on, Cat, go for it with the claws, now the teeth. You've got him now, Dog. Grind those jaws. Don't growl, it'll weaken your grip. Give it a shake, Cat, it'll throw him. Hang on in there, Dog . . .' and so on.

Dog and Cat start getting tired. Cat has an idea.

While he's hanging on with his claws, he shouts to Monkey, 'Say, Monkey, any chance you could help us here? Couldn't you share it out between us so we each had equal parts?'

Monkey calls back, 'I'd love to. We'll just set up some scales to make sure everything's fair, right?'

So Cat and Dog let go of the meat and Monkey sets about making some scales with wood and leaves and vines. It's perfect.

'Right,' says Monkey, 'let's give it a try.'

He tears the meat in half and puts half on each side of the scales.

'Ah,' says Monkey, 'you can see it's not quite a proper half because one side's gone down lower than the other. That means that the meat on that side is just a teeny bit too much. I tell you what, I'll just nibble a bit off that side to even it up, OK?'

Monkey chews a bit off the heavier side

and puts the two bits back on the balance.
Cat and Dog are very impressed at his
cleverness.

'Oh, whoops!' says Monkey. 'I must have
chewed a bit too much off that side, because
look – it's the other side that's lower now. I
tell you what, I'll just nibble an incy little
bit off there and it'll be ready to share out.'

Monkey chews a bit off the heavier side
again and puts the two bits back on the balance. Cat and Dog lean forward waiting for
the balance to settle. But now the first side
goes down again.

'Oh no,' says Monkey. 'Well, look at that.
I still haven't got it quite right. But we're
nearly there, believe me. You're not long off
having your feast, fellers.'

Monkey chews a bit more off the meat
and puts the two bits back.

'Here we go,' says Monkey, 'this is it.'

Once again Cat and Dog get ready to eat
but yet again one side goes down lower.

'Oh dear, oh dear, oh dear,' says Monkey.
'This isn't going quite as I planned. But we
must get it right, or you two will argue
about this for years, eh?'

Monkey takes another bite off the meat and to tell the truth, there isn't much left. Now, when he puts the two bits on the balance, one is mostly bone and the other is just a sliver of meat. Monkey is most upset.

'This isn't going right at all, is it?'

At that he stuffs the last bit of meat into his mouth, tosses the bone away and leaps up into the tree.

There, he wipes his mouth and calls down to Dog and Cat, 'Say fellers, any time you've got something to share out, just bring it along to me and I'll be glad to help you again.'

Mighty Mountain and the Three Strong Women

IRENE HEDLUND – ENGLISH VERSION BY JUDITH ELKIN

Many years ago in a small village in Japan, a huge baby was born. He was so big that everyone called him Baby Mountain.

By the time he was twelve, he was the biggest, strongest boy in the school and the wrestling champion of the whole village. The people in the village were proud of their enormous champion and called him Mighty Mountain.

One warm autumn day, Mighty Mountain decided he must leave the village. He would go to the capital and become a famous wrestler. Every year, the Emperor held a grand wrestling match to find the strongest man in all Japan. Mighty Mountain was sure that he could win.

It was a long walk to the capital and Mighty Mountain strode along, humming to himself. At each step, the ground shook, birds fell from the trees, and animals scurried away in terror.

Mighty Mountain didn't even notice. He was too busy thinking how wonderful he was. Everyone loved him because he was so big and strong. He was quite sure that he was the best-looking wrestler in all Japan, but of course he was far too modest to boast about it.

Just then, Mighty Mountain noticed a girl filling her bucket with water. She was very pretty, with pink cheeks, shining black hair and sparkling eyes.

As the girl climbed on to the footpath in front of him, Mighty Mountain grinned to himself. What fun it would be to tickle her and make her spill the water. Perhaps he could walk home with her and help her to carry the bucket.

Mighty Mountain crept up behind the girl and poked a giant finger in her side. The girl squealed and giggled, but she didn't spill the water. Then, before Mighty Mountain could move away, she trapped his massive hand under her arm.

Mighty Mountain was delighted. Playful as well as pretty, he thought. He tried to pull his hand away, but it wouldn't budge. He pulled harder.

'Let me go,' he laughed. 'You're very strong for a girl, but I don't want to hurt you.'

'Oh, don't worry about that,' giggled the girl, 'I love strong men. Try pulling harder.' She smiled sweetly at him.

But the harder he pulled and tugged, the tighter the girl's grip seemed to get. She began to walk on, dragging the wrestler behind her.

'Please, let me go,' he begged. 'I'm Mighty Mountain, strongest and bravest of all the wrestlers and I'm on my way to

take part in the Emperor's Wrestling
Match.'

'Oh, you must come and meet Grandma,
then. You seem tired. Let me carry you to
our house.'

'Certainly not. Just let me go!'

The girl stopped and seemed to look
right inside him.

'I'm sure you're a good wrestler,' she said
kindly, 'but what will you do when you meet
someone who is really strong? You've got
three months before the wrestling match. I
know becuase Grandma thought of taking
part. If you come home with me now, we
could make you into the strongest man in all
Japan. Otherwise, you will only spend all
your time in bad company and lose what
little strength you've got.'

'I don't need help from you, or Grandma,
or anyone else,' roared Mighty Mountain, but
a tiny shadow of doubt had begun to creep
into his mind. He *was* feeling tired and his
knees had gone quite weak. If he refused to go
with the girl, she might easily break his arm or
throw him down the steep mountainside.

He nodded wearily. The girl let him go.

He peered down miserably at his red, swollen hand and wondered what he had let himself in for.

They came at last to a small thatched hut high up in the mountains. The girl pointed to two tiny feet in the doorway. Grandma was having her afternoon nap.

Round the corner of the hut came a woman carrying a cow on one shoulder. It was the girl's mother, back from working in the fields. When she caught sight of them, she put the cow down and hurriedly brushed the cowhair off her clothes.

'The poor cow gets sore feet, if I let her walk on the stony paths,' she explained to the astonished Mighty Mountain. 'Who is this nice young man, Kuniko?'

Kuniko told her. The two women walked around the wrestler, looking him up and down. Mighty Mountain giggled nervously and puffed out his chest and arms to show his huge muscles.

'Mm,' said Mother, 'he looks delicate. He needs some proper food.'

Then Kuniko called Grandma. She shouted very loudly because Grandma was a little deaf. The tiny feet started to kick furiously.

'All right, all right, I'm coming!'

A tiny, very wrinkled, toothless old lady shuffled out, leaning heavily on a stick. She stumbled over the roots of the great oak tree in the yard.

'Ow . . . ow . . . ow . . .' she muttered. 'My eyes aren't what they used to be. That's the third time this week I've bumped into that silly old tree.'

She put her thin arms round the trunk and pulled it straight out of the ground.

'Throw it away, dear,' she said to her daughter, 'I don't think my poor old back could manage it. Mind it doesn't get in anyone's way. You know how clumsy you are.'

Kuniko's mother threw the tree. It flew through the air like a rocket, getting smaller and smaller until it landed on the far mountainside.

Mighty Mountain could stand no more. His face went pale, his eyes glazed over and his massive legs trembled. Suddenly, with a terrific thump, he crumpled to the ground.

Mighty Mountain had fainted.

Grandma noticed him for the first time, as he crashed at her feet. 'Who's this?' she cackled.

Kuniko gently cradled Mighty Mountain in her arms. 'Poor weak man,' she whispered. 'Do you think we could get him ready for the ring in only three months?'

Grandma sighed. 'Well, it's not long,' she said, 'and he's a feeble-looking fellow.' She bent down and flung him over her shoulder. Leaning heavily on her stick, she hobbled back into the hut and threw him on the bed.

The next day, the three women set to work.

Very early every morning, Kuniko dragged Mighty Mountain out of bed and made him bathe in the icy stream. Each day, Mother boiled his rice in less and less water, until he could eat food no ordinary man could even chew. Grandma made him work harder and harder and carry heavier and heavier loads.

Every evening, Mighty Mountain practised wrestling with grandma. Grandma was so old and frail that she couldn't do him too much harm. The exercise might even help her rheumatism.

As the days grew colder and colder and autumn turned to winter, Mighty Mountain got stronger and stronger, almost without noticing. Soon he could pull up trees almost as easily as Grandma could. He could even throw them, but not very far.

Before wrestling practice, Mighty Mountain stamped his foot on the ground. Then the villagers down below looked up at the winter sky and wondered why the thunder was rumbling round the mountains so late in the year.

One evening, Mighty Mountain managed to hold Grandma down on the ground for half a minute.

Grandma's face broke into a thousand wrinkles as she cackled loudly. Kuniko shrieked with excitement and hugged him, almost breaking his ribs. Mother slapped him on the back, making his eyes water.

They all agreed that Mighty Mountain was ready to take part in the Emperor's Wrestling Match.

'We want you to take the cow,' said Mother. 'Sell her and buy yourself a belt of silk, the thickest and heaviest you can find.

If you wear it when you greet the Emperor, it will remind you of us and bring you luck.'

Mighty Mountain looked worried. 'I can't take the cow. How will you plough the fields?'

Grandma almost fell over laughing. Kuniko giggled, 'We don't use the cow for work. Mother is five times stronger than any cow. We only keep the cow because she's got such beautiful brown eyes.'

'She's very pretty,' agreed Mother, 'but it's hard work carrying her down to the valley every day to find grass.'

'Then if I earn any money at the Wrestling Match, you shall have it.'

Kuniko blushed, 'Oh, no,' she said, 'we can't take money from a stranger.'

Mighty Mountain grinned at her, bowed low to Grandma and asked if he could marry Kuniko and become one of the family.

Kuniko clapped her hands with joy. Grandma and Mother pretended to give the matter deep and serious consideration, then, with big smiles, they agreed. 'We'll even let you beat us at wrestling sometimes.'

The very next morning, Mighty Mountain tied his hair in a fancy topknot, thanked Mother, threw Grandma up in the air just for fun, and playfully tickled Kuniko.

He ran off down the mountain carrying the cow and waving until he could no longer see the three women.

At the first town he came to, Mighty Mountain sold the cow. She had never worked, so she was good and fat, and fetched a high price. With the money, he bought the thickest and heaviest silk belt he could find. Then he headed towards the capital.

Mighty Mountain hardly noticed the cold as he crunched through the snow in his bare feet. He was too busy thinking of Kuniko and Mother and Grandma.

When he reached the Emperor's Palace, he found that the other wrestlers were already there. They were lazing about, preening themselves, eating large bowls of soft rice, telling fantastic stories and comparing their enormous weights and their huge stomachs. No one took any notice of Mighty Mountain.

In the Palace Yard, the ladies-in-waiting and courtiers waited for the wrestling to begin. They wore layers and layers of clothes, so heavy with gold and embroidery that they could hardly move. The ladies-in-waiting wore thick white make-up, and the false eyebrows painted high on their foreheads made them look surprised all the time.

The Emperor sat as still as a statue and all alone behind a screen. He was far too aloof and dignified to be seen by ordinary people. The wrestling bored him. He much preferred reading and writing poetry and hoped the wrestling would soon be over.

The first match was between Mighty Mountain and Balloon Belly, a wrestler who was famous for his gigantic stomach.

With great ceremony, the two wrestlers threw a little salt into the ring to drive away evil spirits. Then they stood, legs apart, facing each other.

Balloon Belly rippled his enormous stomach then raised his foot and stamped the ground with a terrific crash. He glared at Mighty Mountain, as if to say, 'Beat that, weakling!'

Mighty Mountain glared back at Balloon Belly, thought of Grandma and stamped his foot. It sounded like a clap of thunder. The ground shook and Balloon Belly floated out of the ring like a giant green soap bubble. He landed with a thud in front of the Emperor's screen.

'The Earth God is angry,' Balloon Belly stammered, bowing low to the screen, 'I think there's something wrong with the salt. I had better not wrestle again this year.'

Five other wrestlers thought the Earth God might be angry with them, too, and decided not to wrestle.

When the next competitor was ready, Mighty Mountain was careful not to stamp his foot too hard. He just picked his opponent up round the waist and carried him out of the ring.

With a polite bow, Mighty Mountain placed the wrestler in front of the Emperor's screen. Then, one by one, he did exactly the same with all the other wrestlers.

The ladies-in-waiting looked more surprised than ever as they giggled delightedly behind their fans.

The Emperor's shoulders heaved with silent laughter and the plume on his head-dress wobbled in a most undignified manner. He hadn't seen anything so funny for years. He put one royal finger through the screen and waggled it at the wrestlers who were sitting on the ground blubbering. He gave orders for Mighty Mountain to receive all the prize money.

The Emperor congratulated Mighty Mountain. 'But,' he whispered, 'I don't think you had better take part again next year. We don't want to upset these poor babies any more.' He looked at the heap of wrestlers and started giggling again.

Mighty Mountain agreed quite happily. He had decided that he would much rather be a farmer anyway, and he hurried off back to Kuniko.

Kuniko saw him coming from a long way off and ran to meet him. She hugged him carefully, then picked him up and carried him and the heavy bag of money halfway up the mountain. Then she put him down and let him carry her the rest of the way home.

The name of Mighty Mountain was soon

forgotten in the capital. But the Emperor never really enjoyed another wrestling match and was always glad when it was over and he could get back to his poetry.

Now and again, the people in the village down below feel the earth shake and hear thunder rumbling round the mountains. But it's only Mighty Mountain and Grandma practising their wrestling.

Tsipporah

ADÈLE GERAS

Here is something I've noticed: as soon as candles are lit, as soon as night falls, my grandmother, my parents and all my uncles and aunts start telling stories, and the stories are often frightening, meant to send small shivers up and down every bit of you. When the grown-ups talk, I listen. I never tell them *my* frightening story, even though it is true. They wouldn't believe me.

A few weeks after my eighth birthday, my grandmother took me to visit her friend

Naomi. Why, I wanted to know, had I not seen this friend before?

'I never take very young children to see her. She might frighten them. The way she looks, I mean,' said my grandmother.

I imagined a witch, a giantess, or some monster I couldn't quite describe. I said, 'What's the matter with her?'

'Nothing's the matter with her. She's very old, that's all.'

I laughed. 'But you're very old and I'm not scared of you.'

My grandmother said, 'Compared with Naomi, I'm a rosebud, I promise you. Wait and see.'

She was quite right. Naomi was ancient. Her head was like a walnut, or a prune, perhaps, with eyes and a mouth set into it. She wore a headscarf and I was glad of that. I was sure she was bald underneath it. She sat in a chair pulled up to the table, drinking black coffee and smoking horrible-smelling cigarettes. She spoke in a voice like machinery that needed oiling. After I was introduced to her, I was supposed to sit quietly while the ladies chatted. I couldn't think of anything worse, so I said to my grandmother, 'May I go out into the courtyard for a while? I'll just look at things. I promise not to leave the house.'

My grandmother agreed, and I stepped out of Naomi's dark dining-room into the sunshine. The rooms Naomi lived in could have been called a flat, I suppose, but it wasn't a flat in a modern block. It was in a part of Jerusalem where the houses were built around a central courtyard, and four or five families shared the building. In this courtyard there were pots filled with geraniums outside one door, and some watermelon seeds drying on a brass tray outside another. A small, sand-coloured cat with limp, white paws was sleeping in a patch of shade. Naomi's rooms were on the upper storey of the house. It was about three o'clock in the afternoon. All the shutters were closed. Perhaps everyone who lived here was old and taking an afternoon nap. The sun pressed down on the butter-yellow flagstones of the courtyard, and the walls glittered in the heat. Suddenly I heard a noise in the middle of all the silence: a cooing, a whirring of small wings. I turned round to look, and there, almost within reach of my hand, was a white dove sitting on the balcony railing.

'How lovely!' I said to it. 'You're a lovely bird then! Where have you come from?'

The bird cocked its head, and looked exactly as though it were about to answer, then it changed its mind and in a blur of white feathers, it flew off the railing and was gone. I leaned over to look for it in the courtyard, and thought I saw it, just there, on a step. I ran down the stairs after it, but it was nowhere to be seen.

A girl of about my age was standing beside a pot of geraniums.

Where had she come from? She wore a white dress which fell almost to her ankles. I thought, She must be very religious. I knew that very devout Jews wore old-fashioned clothes.

'Have you seen a white dove?' I asked her. 'It was up there a moment ago.'

The girl smiled. She said, 'Sometimes I dream that I'm a dove. Do you believe in dreams? I do. My name is Tsipporah, which

means "bird", so of course I feel exactly like
a bird sometimes. What do you feel like?'

I didn't know what to say. I was thinking, This girl is mad. My name is Rachel,
which means 'ewe lamb', but I never feel
woolly or frisky. My cousin is called Arieh,
which means 'lion', and he's not a bit
tawny or fierce. I said, 'I just feel like
myself.'

'Then you're lucky,' said Tsipporah.
'Sometimes I think I will turn into a bird
at any moment. In fact, look, it's happening . . . feathers . . . white feathers on my
arms . . .'

I did look. She held out her arms and
cocked her head, and I blinked in the sunlight which all at once was shining straight
into my eyes and dazzling me . . . but in the
light I could see . . . I think I saw, though
it's hard to remember exactly, a flapping, a
vibration of wings, and the krr-krr of soft
dove-sounds filling every space in my head.
I closed my eyes and opened them again
slowly. Tsipporah had disappeared. I could
see a white bird over on the other side of the
courtyard, and I ran towards it calling,

'Tsipporah, if it's you, come back . . . come back and tell me!'

The dove launched itself into the air, and flew up and up and over the roof and away, and I followed it with my eyes until the speck that it was had vanished into the wide pale sky. I felt weak, dizzy with heat. I climbed slowly back to Naomi's rooms, thinking, Tsipporah must have hidden from me. She must be a child who lives in the building and likes playing tricks.

On the way home, my grandmother started telling me one of her stories. Sometimes I don't listen properly when she starts on a tale of how this person is related to that one, but she was talking about Naomi when she was young, and that was so hard to imagine that I was fascinated.

'Of course,' my grandmother said, 'she was never quite the same after Tsipporah died.'

'Who,' I asked, suddenly cold in the sunlight, 'is Tsipporah?'

'Naomi's twin sister. She died of diphtheria when they were eight. A terrible tragedy. But Tsipporah was strange.'

'How, strange?'

'Naomi told me stories . . . you would hardly believe them if I told you. I know I never did.'

'Tell me,' I said. 'I'll believe them.'

'Naomi always said her sister could turn herself into a bird just by wishing it.'

'A white dove,' I said. 'She turned herself into a white dove and flew away.'

My grandmother looked at me sharply.

'I've told you this story before, haven't I?'

'Yes,' I said, even though, of course, she never had. I didn't tell her I had seen Tsipporah. I didn't want to frighten her, so I said nothing about it.

Now, every time I see a white dove, I wonder if it's her, Tsipporah, or perhaps some other girl who stretched her wings out one day, looking for the sky.

The Palace of Boundless Cold

ROSALIND KERVEN

Once a boy found an injured swallow lying by the side of the road. It lay twittering pitifully, and trying helplessly to move its broken wing. The boy picked it up and carried it home. There he laid it in a box lined with a scrap of old silk, and cared for it gently and kindly for many days.

In the fullness of time, the bird's wing healed. The boy's joy at having nursed it better was tinged with sadness, for he knew now that it must fly away and become wild again.

But the swallow did not forget him. A few days later, it came back to his house and waited on the doorstep until he came out. In its beak, it carried a yellow pumpkin seed. It dropped this at the boy's feet. Then it flew away for good.

The boy planted the seed in his garden. Very quickly, it grew into a strong plant. It flowered, and then began to form a single fruit. This pumpkin seemed to grow fatter and firmer almost as he watched it.

When at last it was ripe, he picked it and cut it open. He was astonished to find a pile of gold and silver coins tumbling out.

It did not take long for news of what had happened to spread right round the village. Everyone was pleased: his family, though hard working, had always been rather poor, and all this money would make things easier for them. Besides, it was good to know that saving even such a tiny, insignificant creature, might earn a lucky reward from Heaven.

But in every village there is always a bad apple. Here, it was another lad, about the same age as the first, who happened to live almost next door to him. To put it bluntly, he was terribly greedy, and burned with envy when he heard about the gold and silver. He decided to waste no time in trying to win something similar for himself.

So he found a small bird of his own, and threw a stone at it – deliberately. The poor thing fell down and broke both its legs: it must have been in terrible pain. The boy picked it up and took it inside. From this point, he made a great public fuss and show of nursing it back to health.

As soon as the bird was recovered, he sent it flying off. Then he settled down to wait for his reward.

Sure enough, a few days later, it returned to him and dropped a pumpkin seed at his feet.

The boy rushed to plant it. Each day as it grew and developed into a fruit, he gloated over it, imagining the fortune that would soon be his. The other villagers tutted and shook their heads over him, but he took no notice.

At last the fruit was ripe. With trembling

hands, he picked it and cut it open on the spot.

The two halves split open, as they had done for the first boy; but there was no treasure inside this one. Instead, out stepped a stern old gentleman with a long white beard and the formal robes of a government official.

He stared coldly at the boy.

'So,' he exclaimed, 'you are the person who has such a longing for gold and silver, eh? Well, if that is what you want so badly, you had better come along this way with me.'

He seized the lad by the hand. Just then, the runners of the pumpkin began to grow and turn into a towering ladder that led straight up into the sky. Pulling the boy behind him, the gentleman stepped briskly on to the bottom rung and began to climb steadily up. All the while, the wretched boy struggled to be free, but the stern old gentleman held him in an iron grip.

Only once, he dared to look down. To his horror, he saw that below them, the rungs of the ladder had shrivelled up and fallen off: there was no escape.

On and on they climbed, into darkness. Then at last they stepped off the ladder, and entered an extraordinary place that was dazzlingly bright, yet bitterly cold.

Now they set off along a long straight empty road made of white jade.

'Where . . . where are we, Sir?' whispered the boy, as he tried to catch his breath.

'On the moon of course.'

'The moon! Oh! And . . . please, Sir, where are we going to?'

'To the Palace of Boundless Cold.'

At last they reached the road's end. Before them stood a vast building. Its walls were solid gold. Its windows were pure silver.

The old gentleman stopped.

'I trust that this satisfies you? There is more gold and silver here than most people could ever dream of.'

The boy looked around. Everything was utterly still and silent. There seemed to be no one else, and nothing alive. The coldness of the air was rapidly seeping into him, freezing his bones, his blood and his very heart.

'Please, Sir,' he said, 'I think . . . there has been a mistake. I . . . I . . . Can I go home now?'

'Oh oh!' exclaimed the stern old gentleman. 'So you have decided to change your mind, eh?' He gave a dry laugh that sent a shiver down the boy's spine. 'Well, hmmm . . . I might consider letting you off after all; but first you must do a little job for me.'

He led the boy round a corner of the palace to what seemed at a glance to be a small cinnamon tree. But when he examined it more carefully, the boy saw that its trunk and branches were formed of gold, and its leaves were all glittering precious stones.

The stern old gentleman handed him a silver axe.

'You may use this to try and cut down the tree,' he said. 'If you succeed, then I will allow you to go home at once; and even to take the tree with you. You can see for yourself, it is laden with enough riches to satisfy your greed for the rest of your life.'

'Supposing I don't want to be rich any more, Sir?' asked the boy hoarsely. 'Supposing I don't want the tree?'

'You should have thought of that before you deliberately injured that innocent little bird,' replied the old gentleman. 'It is too late to change your fate now. So take this axe at once, if you please, and begin the task you have been set.'

With a heavy sigh, the boy took the axe, swung it back and at once cut a large notch into the golden trunk.

'This is easy after all,' he thought to himself. But just then, he felt a dreadful pain in his shoulders.

Swinging round, he found that he was being attacked by an enormous white cockerel.

'Go away!' he yelled, and chased it off with his axe.

He returned to the golden tree, hoping another blow or two might fell it. But to his horror, the notch he had already cut into the trunk had completely disappeared.

Again he struck it with his axe. Again he was attacked by the fierce white cockerel.

Again he chased it away, and again he found that the mark he had made with the axe had totally disappeared.

And again, and again, and again . . .

He's still stuck up there today, frozen into the silvery light of the Palace of Boundless Cold. The stern old gentleman is still up there with him, watching in icy silence as the boy sweats away at his impossible task.

So if ever you feel like playing a mean trick to get rich quick – look up at the moon and remember him!

Secrets

ANITA DESAI

One morning, at school, Rohan got every single sum wrong. Then he dropped a bottle of ink on the floor and it splashed on to his teacher's white canvas shoes. When he made a face behind his teacher's back, he was seen. So he had to be punished.

'Here, take this letter to your father and go home,' his teacher said, after writing a long and angry letter. 'Let him punish you as well.'

Rohan tried to look too proud to care, and picked up his books and walked out of the school yard and up the narrow city lane. But once he reached the big grey banyan tree that was the only tree in the lane, and found that the cobbler who usually sat under it, mending broken old shoes, was not there, he sat down in its shade, hiding himself in the folds of the great trunk, and sobbed a little with anger. He had not been able to get his sums right although he had tried. He had dropped the ink bottle by accident and not to spoil the teacher's white shoes. Perhaps it was bad of him to pull a face but how could he help it when things were going so badly? Now he was afraid to go home and hand the letter to his father, who would be very angry and beat him. He sometimes did, and often scolded him.

So Rohan hid there in the folds of the grey tree-trunk, and poked with a stick at the seeds dropped on the ground by the parrots that ate the red berries of the tree. He was so angry and afraid that he poked and poked with the stick till he had dug quite a deep hole in the dust. In that hole he found a little grey lump of rubber – a plain piece of rubber that some other schoolboy might have dropped there long ago. He picked it up and rolled it about between his fingers.

'I wish it were a magic rubber,' he said, sobbing a little. 'I would rub out the whole school, like this – like this –' and he stepped out to look down the lane at the boys' school that stood at the end of it, and angrily rubbed at the air with the grey lump of rubber.

Then he stopped, his hand still in mid-air, his mouth still open, and his hair began to stand up on his head as it did on his neighbour's cat's back when she saw his dog.

Something very, very strange had happened. The school had vanished. He had really rubbed it out! The tall, three-storeyed house on its left, with its latticed balconies and green roof, was still there, and on the other side the tin-roofed warehouse where timber was stacked stood there too, but in between them, where the school had been, there was now a patch of earth. There was no white school building, no deep verandas, no dusty playground, no high grey wall and not a single schoolboy. There was just a square of bare brown earth between the other buildings, all quiet and still now in the heat of the afternoon.

Rohan's knees were shaking. He ran a little way down the road to see better but still could find nothing but a blank where the school had once been. Then he felt so afraid of the vanished school that he ran back up the lane as fast as he could, snatched up his books and the terrible rubber from among the roots of the banyan, and ran into the road where he lived. He hurried up the stairs at the side of the little yellow house to their room on the roof where his mother hung the clothes to dry and his father stacked old boxes and bicycle tyres.

His mother was alone at home. She was kneading dough in a big brass pan. The fire was not yet lit. 'You're early,' she said, in surprise. 'I haven't any food ready for you yet. But you can go and break up an old box and get me some wood to light the fire. I'll warm some milk for you. Hurry up, don't look so sulky,' she said, and began to roll and thump the dough in the pan, roll and thump, roll and thump, so she did not see the face Rohan made as he went out to pull an old crate to pieces and bring in an arm-load of packing-case wood.

He came in and threw it all into the grate with such force that the ashes and grit flew up and settled on all the pots and pans, and the dough and the neat floor as well.

His mother was so angry, she shouted, 'What's the matter with you, you rascal? Look what you've done! What a mess you've made. Now go and fetch the broom and sweep it up at once.'

'I won't sweep,' he shouted back, as loudly as though there were a devil in him, shouting for him.

She was still more angry. 'I won't sweep it up either. Let it lie there, and then your father will see it when he comes home,' she said.

Then Rohan felt so afraid that he held up the magic rubber and cried, 'I won't let you do that. I won't let him see it. I'll – I'll rub you all out,' and he swept through the air with that little grey lump of rubber, as hard as he could. He shut his eyes tight because his face was all screwed up with anger, and when he opened them the whole house with the unlit fire, the brass pan, the glass of milk and even his mother had vanished. There was only the roof-top, blazing in the afternoon sun, littered with empty tins and old tyres at the edges but quite, quite bare in the middle.

Now Rohan did not have a home or a mother or even a glass of milk. His mouth hung open, he was so frightened by what he had done. Then he turned and ran down the stairs as fast as he could, so that his father would not come and find him standing alone on the empty roof-top.

He heard an excited bark and saw it was his dog Kalo, who had been sleeping in the shade of an overturned basket in a corner of the roof-top, but had heard him run down the stairs and followed him. Kalo was frightened, too, at the way their room had disappeared and the roof-top left standing empty, so he was running along behind Rohan, barking with fright.

Rohan felt afraid that the people who

lived in the yellow house would come out and see what had happened, so he shouted 'Go back Kalo! Go back!' But Kalo ran towards him, his long black ears flapping as he ran. So Rohan rubbed the air with his rubber again and screamed, 'I don't want you! Go away!' and Kalo vanished. His round paw marks were still to be seen in the dust of the road. A little trail of dust was still hanging in the hot, still air of that dreadful afternoon, but Kalo the dog had vanished.

And someone had seen. An old man who traded in empty tins and bottles had just started his evening round and, while shouting 'Tin and bo –' stopped short and stared till Rohan, rubbing in the air with his rubber again, shouted, 'You can't see! You mustn't see!' and rubbed him out. That old man with his grey beard and big sack of clanking tins and bottles just disappeared as Kalo had.

Then Rohan turned and ran even faster. He ran into the big road that went round the mosque. Just in time he remembered that he might meet his father there, for he had a cycle repair shop at the foot of the mosque steps. So he whirled around again. He kept going in circles, as if he were a little mad. At last he ran to the banyan tree, climbed over its roots into a cleft between two folds of the huge trunk and hid there, trembling.

'I'll hide this terrible rubber,' he said at last. 'I'll put it back in the hole and never, never take it out again.' With shaking fingers he scraped more dust from the little hole he had dug earlier, in order to bury the rubber.

As he scraped and dug with trembling fingers, he found something else in the hole. At first he saw only one end of it – it was long and yellow. He dug harder and found it was a pencil. Quite a new pencil – he could see no one had used it before, though it looked old from being buried in the earth. He stopped crying and trembling as he wondered who could have buried a pencil here, and whether it was a magic pencil as the rubber was a magic one. He had to try it and see.

First he dropped the rubber into the hole

and covered it up. Then he held up the pencil and pointed it at the bare patch of earth where the school had once stood between the warehouse and the green-roofed house. Very, very carefully he drew a picture of his old white school building in the air. He did it so carefully that he seemed to see the grey lines forming before his eyes. Then he blinked: the grey-white building really *was* there now. Or was it only a picture in his mind? Quickly he drew the verandas, the playground, the high wall, and then the little matchstick figures of a line of schoolboys rushing out of the front gate, the lane filling with them, and saw them leaping and running with their satchels flying behind them.

He stood up and ran a little way down the lane, out of the shade of the mysteriously whispering banyan tree. Now, in the clear sunlight, he could see the school quite plainly again, alive and noisy with children set free from their lessons. He stood there till he saw the teacher come out on his bicycle. Then he turned and ran the other way up the lane.

He stood in the middle of the dusty road and quickly, quickly, drew a picture of a little black dog in the air, as well as he could. He was still working on the long plumed tail when he heard Kalo bark, and saw him bounce down on to the road on his four feet and come pelting towards him.

As he came closer, Rohan saw he had missed out the jagged edge of Kalo's ear where it had been torn in a dog-fight. He was careful to add that so Kalo would be exactly as he had been before, scarred and dusty and wild with happiness. Kalo stood still, waiting for him to finish.

When it was done, he shouted 'Kalo! Kalo!' and patted him hastily, then went on busily with his pencil, drawing the old, bearded tin-and-bottle man. He was just drawing the big, bulging sack when he heard the cracked voice cry '-o-ttle man!' and there he was, shuffling down the road and blinking a little in the bright light.

Then Rohan and his dog ran home, up the stairs to the empty roof-top. There, leaning against the low wall, his tongue between his teeth and his eyes narrowed,

Rohan drew a picture of his home as well as he could. Even when he could see it quite plainly, the little whitewashed room with its arched windows and pigeon-roost on the flat roof, he went on drawing. He drew a picture of his mother kneading dough in a pan, the fire, the glass of milk and even the broom in the corner of the room. Then he went in and found them all there, just as he had drawn them. But he saw one mistake he had made in his drawing – he had coloured his mother's hair black and left out the grey strands over her ears. She had remained stiff, lifeless. He stood in the doorway, rubbing gently at the unnatural darkness of her hair till it showed the grey he knew. He realized you cannot draw a picture out of desperation, or with careless speed. It took care, attention, time.

When he had finished, his mother moved, looked up at him. 'There's your milk,' she said quietly, 'drink it up.'

He nodded. 'I'll sweep up a bit first,' he said, and went to fetch the broom. He swept and he swept, enjoying the work that he had not wanted to do at first, till he heard his father arrive, lean his bicycle against the wall and lock it, then come slowly up the stairs.

Rohan ran out, shouting 'Look, I found a pencil and a rubber on the road today.' He wanted so much to tell his father all about it and ask him how it happened, but he did not dare.

His father was looking tired. 'Why don't you sit quietly and draw something?' he said, as he went in for his tea.

Rohan nodded and went to fetch a piece of paper. Then he sat on the top step and spread out the paper and drew. He was not sure if the magic pencil would draw an ordinary picture. It did. Using it very, very carefully now, he drew a picture of Kalo.

When his father saw it, he beamed. He had never seen a picture as good. Rohan showed it to his mother too, and she was so pleased she pinned it on the wall, next to the calendar.

His father said, 'I didn't know you could draw so well. Your teacher never told us. You should draw a picture for him.'

Rohan spent the whole evening drawing

with the magic pencil. He took the drawings to school next day, and his teacher was so pleased with them that he forgot to ask for an answer to his angry letter of the day before. He gave Rohan good paper and time to draw every day.

Rohan drew so much that the magic pencil was soon worn to a stub. Instead of throwing it away like an ordinary pencil, he took it down to the banyan tree and buried it in the earth at its roots where he had hidden the lump of rubber. As he walked away he worried about whether he would be able to draw as well with an ordinary pencil bought at the staionery shop near the school gate. But he had had so much practice now, and become so good an artist, that he found he could do as good a drawing with the new pencil he bought as with the magic one.

He became so famous in that town that people came from miles away to see the pictures his mother pinned to the walls of their house. They went to the school and asked the teacher about him. No one knew how he had learnt to draw and paint so well without any lessons or help. Even when he became a great artist, whose name was known all over the land, Rohan did not tell anyone the story. That was his secret – and the banyan tree's, and they kept it to themselves as secrets should be kept.

A Necklace of Raindrops

JOAN AIKEN

A man called Mr Jones and his wife lived near the sea. One stormy night Mr Jones was in his garden when he saw the holly tree by his gate begin to toss and shake.

A voice cried, 'Help me! I'm stuck in the tree! Help me, or the storm will go on all night.'

Very surprised, Mr Jones walked down to the tree. In the middle of it was a tall man with a long grey cloak, and a long grey beard, and the brightest eyes you ever saw.

'Who are you?' Mr Jones said. 'What are you doing in my holly tree?'

'I got stuck in it, can't you see? Help me out, or the storm will go on all night. I am the North Wind, and it is my job to blow the storm away.'

So Mr Jones helped the North Wind out of the holly tree. The North Wind's hands were as cold as ice.

'Thank you,' said the North Wind. 'My cloak is torn, but never mind. You have helped me, so now I will do something for you.'

'I don't need anything,' Mr Jones said. 'My wife and I have a baby girl, just born, and we are as happy as any two people in the world.'

'In that case,' said the North Wind, 'I will be the baby's godfather. My birthday present to her will be this necklace of raindrops.'

From under his grey cloak he pulled out a fine, fine silver chain. On the chain were three bright, shining drops.

'You must put it round the baby's neck,' he said. 'The raindrops will not wet her, and they will not come off. Every year, on her birthday, I will bring her another drop. When she has four drops she will stay dry, even if she goes out in the hardest rainstorm. And when she has five drops no thunder or lightning can harm her. And when she has six drops she will not be blown away, even by the strongest wind. And when she has seven raindrops she will be able to swim the deepest river. And when she has eight raindrops she will be able to swim the widest sea. And when she has nine raindrops she will be able to make the rain stop raining if she claps her hands. And when she has ten raindrops she will be able to make it start raining if she blows her nose.'

'Stop, stop!' cried Mr Jones. 'That is quite enough for one little girl!'

'I was going to stop anyway,' said the North Wind. 'Mind, she must never take the chain off, or it might bring bad luck. I must be off, now, to blow away the storm. I shall be back on her next birthday, with the fourth raindrop.'

And he flew away up into the sky, pushing the clouds before him so that the moon and stars could shine out.

Mr Jones went into his house and put the chain with the three raindrops round the neck of the baby, who was called Laura.

A year soon went by, and when the North Wind came back to the little house by the sea, Laura was able to crawl about, and to play with her three bright, shining rain-drops. But she never took the chain off.

When the North Wind had given Laura her fourth raindrop she could not get wet, even if she was out in the hardest rain. Her mother would put her out in the garden in her pram, and people passing on the road would say, 'Look at that poor little baby, left out in all this rain. She will catch cold!'

But little Laura was quite dry, and quite happy, playing with the raindrops and waving to her godfather the North Wind as he flew over.

Next year he brought her her fifth rain-drop. And the year after that, the sixth. And the year after that, the seventh. Now Laura could not be harmed by the worst storm, and if she fell into a pond or river she float-ed like a feather. And when she had eight raindrops she was able to swim across the widest sea – but as she was happy at home she had never tried.

And when she had nine raindrops Laura found that she could make the rain stop, by clapping her hands. So there were many, many sunny days by the sea. But Laura did not always clap her hands when it rained, for she loved to see the silver drops come sliding out of the sky.

Now it was time for Laura to go to school. You can guess how the other children loved her! They would call, 'Laura, Laura, make it stop raining, please, so that we can go out to play.'

And Laura always made the rain stop for them.

But there was a girl called Meg who said to herself, 'It isn't fair. Why should Laura have that lovely necklace and be able to stop the rain? Why shouldn't I have it?'

So Meg went to the teacher and said, 'Laura is wearing a necklace.'

Then the teacher said to Laura, 'You must take your necklace off in school, dear. That is the rule.'

'But it will bring bad luck if I take it off,' said Laura.

'Of course it will not bring bad luck. I will put it in a box for you and keep it safe till after school.'

So the teacher put the necklace in a box.

But Meg saw where she put it. And when the children were out playing, and the teacher was having her dinner, Meg went quickly and took the necklace and put it in her pocket.

When the teacher found that the necklace was gone, she was very angry and sad.

'Who has taken Laura's necklace?' she asked.

But nobody answered.

Meg kept her hand tight in her pocket, holding the necklace.

And poor Laura cried all the way home. Her tears rolled down her cheeks like rain as she walked along by the sea.

'Oh,' she cried, 'what will happen when I tell my godfather that I have lost his present?'

A fish put his head out of the water and said, 'Don't cry, Laura dear. You put me back in the sea when a wave threw me on the sand. I will help you find your necklace.'

And a bird flew down and called, 'Don't cry, Laura dear. You saved me when a storm blew me on to your roof and hurt my wing. I will help you find your necklace.'

And a mouse popped his head out of a hole and said, 'Don't cry, Laura dear. You saved me once when I fell in the river. I will help you find your necklace.'

So Laura dried her eyes. 'How will you help me?' she asked.

'I will look under the sea,' said the fish. 'And I will ask my brothers to help me.'

'I will fly about and look in the fields and woods and roads,' said the bird. 'And I will ask all my brothers to help me.'

'I will look in the houses,' said the mouse. 'And I will ask my brothers to look in every corner and closet of every room in the world.'

So they set to work.

While Laura was talking to her three friends, what was Meg doing?

She put on the necklace and walked out in a rainstorm. But the rain made her very wet! And when she clapped her hands to stop it raining, the rain took no notice. It rained harder than ever.

The necklace would only work for its true owner.

So Meg was angry. But she still wore the necklace, until her father saw her with it on.

'Where did you get that necklace?' he asked.

'I found it in the road,' Meg said. Which was not true!

'It is too good for a child,' her father said. And he took it away from her. Meg and her father did not know that a little mouse could see them from a hole in the wall.

The mouse ran to tell his friends that the necklace was in Meg's house. And ten more mice came back with him to drag it away. But when they got there, the necklace was gone. Meg's father had sold it, for a great deal of money, to a silversmith. Two days later, a little mouse saw it in the silver-smith's shop, and ran to tell his friends. But before the mice could come to take it, the silversmith had sold it to a trader who was buying fine and rare presents for the birth-day of the Princess of Arabia.

Then a bird saw the necklace and flew to tell Laura.

'The necklace is on a ship, which is sailing across the sea to Arabia.'

'We will follow the ship,' said the fishes. 'We will tell you which way it goes. Follow us!'

But Laura stood on the edge of the sea.

'How can I swim all that way without my necklace?' she cried.

'I will take you on my back,' said a dolphin. 'You have often thrown me good things to eat when I was hungry.'

So the dolphin took her on his back, and the fishes went on in front, and the birds flew above, and after many days they came to Arabia.

'Now where is the necklace?' called the fishes to the birds.

'The King of Arabia has it. He is going to give it to the Princess for her birthday tomorrow.'

'Tomorrow is my birthday too,' said Laura. 'Oh, what will my godfather say when he comes to give me my tenth raindrop and finds that I have not got the necklace?'

The birds led Laura into the King's garden. And she slept all night under a palm tree. The grass was all dry, and the flowers were all brown, because it was so hot, and had not rained for a year.

Next morning the Princess came into the garden to open her presents. She had many lovely things: a flower that could sing, and a cage full of birds with green and silver feathers; a book that she could read for ever because it had no last page, and a cat who could play cat's cradle; a silver dress of spiderwebs and a gold dress of goldfish scales; a clock with a real cuckoo to tell the time, and a boat made out of a great pink shell. And among all the other presents was Laura's necklace.

When Laura saw the necklace she ran out from under the palm tree and cried, 'Oh, please, that necklace is mine!'

The King of Arabia was angry. 'Who is this girl?' he said. 'Who let her into my garden? Take her away and drop her in the sea!'

But the Princess, who was small and pretty, said, 'Wait a minute, Papa,' and to

Laura she said, 'How do you know it is your necklace?'

'Because my godfather gave it to me! When I am wearing it I can go out in the rain without getting wet, no storm can harm me, I can swim any river and any sea, and I can make the rain stop raining.'

'But can you make it start to rain?' said the King.

'Not yet,' said Laura. 'Not till my god-father gives me the tenth raindrop.'

'If you can make it rain you shall have the necklace,' said the King. 'For we badly need rain in this country.'

But Laura was sad because she could not make it rain till she had her tenth raindrop.

Just then the North Wind came flying into the King's garden.

'There you are, god-daughter!' he said. 'I have been looking all over the world for you, to give you your birthday present. Where is your necklace?'

'The Princess has it,' said poor Laura.

Then the North Wind was angry. 'You should not have taken it off!' he said. And he dropped the raindrop on to the dry grass, where it was lost. Then he flew away. Laura started to cry.

'Don't cry,' said the kind little Princess. 'You shall have the necklace back, for I can see it is yours.' And she put the chain over Laura's head. As soon as she did so, one of Laura's tears ran down and hung on the necklace beside the nine raindrops, making ten. Laura started to smile, she dried her eyes and blew her nose. And, guess what! as soon as she blew her nose, the rain began falling! It rained and it rained, the trees all spread out their leaves, and the flowers stretched their petals, they were so happy to have a drink.

At last Laura clapped her hands to stop the rain.

The King of Arabia was very pleased. 'That is the finest necklace I have ever seen,' he said. 'Will you come and stay with us every year, so that we have enough rain?' And Laura said she would do this.

Then they sent her home in the Princess's boat, made out of a pink shell. And the birds flew overhead, and the fishes swam in front.

'I am happy to have my necklace back,' said Laura. 'But I am even happier to have so many friends.'

What happened to Meg? The mice told the North Wind that she had taken Laura's necklace. And he came and blew the roof off her house and let in the rain, so she was SOAKING WET!

Once There Were No Pandas

MARGARET GREAVES

Long, long ago in China, when the earth and the stars were young, there were none of the black-and-white bears, that the Chinese call *Xiong mao* and that we call 'pandas'. But deep in the bamboo forests lived bears with fur as white and soft and shining as new-fallen snow. The Chinese called them *Bai xiong* which means 'white bear'.

In a small house at the edge of the forest lived a peasant and his wife and their little daughter, Chien-min.

One very hot day, Chien-min was playing alone at the edge of the forest. The green shadow of the trees looked cool as water, and a patch of yellow buttercups shone invitingly.

'They are only *just* inside the forest,' said the little girl to herself. 'It will take only a minute to pick some.'

She slipped in among the trees. But when she had picked her flowers, she looked around puzzled. There were so many small paths! Which one led back to the village?

As she hesitated, something moved and rustled among the leaves nearby. She saw a delicate head with big ears, a slim body dappled with light and shadow. It was one of the small deer of the forest. Chien-min had startled it, and it bounded away between the trees. She tried to follow, hoping it might lead her home. But almost at once it was out of sight, and Chien-min was completely lost.

She began to be frightened. But then she heard another sound – something whimpering not far away. She ran towards the place, forgetting her fear, wanting only to help.

There, close to a big thorny bush,

squatted a very small white bear cub. Every now and then he shook one of his front paws and licked it, then whimpered again.

'Oh, you poor little one!' Chien-min ran over and knelt beside the little bear. 'Don't cry! I'll help you. Let me see it.'

The little cub seemed to understand. He let her take hold of his paw. Between the pads was a very sharp thorn. Chien-min pinched it between her finger and thumb, and very carefully drew it out. The cub rubbed his head against her hands as she stroked him.

A moment later, a huge white bear came crashing through the trees, growling fiercely. But when she saw that the little girl was only playing with her cub, her anger vanished. She licked his paw, then nuzzled Chien-min as if she too were one of her cubs.

The mother bear was so gentle that the child took courage and put her arms round her neck, stroking the soft fur. 'How beautiful you are!' Chien-min said. 'Oh, if only you could show me the way home.'

At once the great bear ambled forward,

grunting to the cub and his new friend to follow. Fearlessly now, Chien-min held on to her thick white coat and very soon found that she was at the edge of the forest again, close to her own home.

From that day on, she often went into the forest. Her parents were happy about it, knowing their daughter was safe under the protection of the great white bear. She met many of the other bears too, and many of their young, but her special friend was always the little cub she had helped. She called him *Niao Niao*, which means 'very soft', because his fur was so fine and beautiful.

The mother bear even showed the little girl her secret home, a den in the hollow of a great tree. Chien-min went there many times, played with the cubs, and learned the ways of the forest. Always the great she-bear led her safely back before nightfall.

One warm spring afternoon, Chien-min was sitting by the hollow tree, watching the cubs at play, when she saw a stealthy movement between the bamboos. A wide, whiskered face. Fierce topaz eyes. Small tufted ears. A glimpse of spotted, silky fur.

Chien-min sprang up, shouting a warning. But she was too late. With bared teeth and lashing tail, the hungry leopard had leaped upon Niao Niao.

Chien-min forgot all her fear in her love for her friend. Snatching up a great stone, she hurled it at the leopard. The savage beast dropped his prey but turned on her, snarling with fury. At the same moment, the she-bear charged through the trees like a thunderbolt.

The leopard backed off, terrified by her anger. But as he turned to run, he struck out at Chien-min with his huge claws, knocking her to the ground.

The bears ran to Chien-min, growling and whining and licking her face, but the little girl never moved. She had saved Niao Niao's life by the loss of her own.

News of her death swept through the forest. From miles away, north, south, east and west, all the white bears gathered to mourn. They wept and whimpered for their lost friend, rubbing their paws in the dust of the earth and wiping the tears from their eyes. As they did so, the wet dust left great black smears across their faces. They beat their paws against their bodies in bitter lamentation, and the wet dust clung to their fur in wide black bands.

But although the bears sorrowed for Chien-min, and her parents and friends mourned her, they were all comforted to know that she was happy. Guan-yin, the beautiful Goddess of Mercy, would give her a special place in heaven, where her selfless love for her friend would always be rewarded.

And from that day to this, there have been no white bears, *Bai xiong*, anywhere in China. Instead there are the great black-and-white bears, *Xiong mao*, that we call 'pandas', still in mourning for their lost friend, Chien-min.

The Gigantic Badness

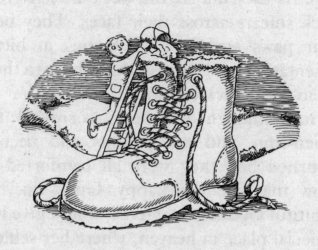

JANET McNEILL

Nobody blamed the Giant for his bigness – a giant can't help being big – but the badness of the Giant was certainly his fault, everyone in the town and countryside was sure about that.

'He's bad, that Giant is,' they grumbled, shaking their heads when they found huge footprints sunk deep on newly sown fields of corn, or hedges squashed flat. 'Never a thought for anyone but himself,' they growled if the Giant sang songs late into the night when everyone else wanted to get to sleep, or when he burned his toast and the smell hung about the air for a couple of days. 'He's a rogue for sure,' they complained, 'if it isn't one thing it's another.' And sometimes they forgot to scold their children for talking with their mouths full, or coming into the house without wiping their feet, or sitting down at the table before their hands were washed, because these were such small badnesses, compared with the enormous outsize badness of the Giant.

Tom was one of the smallest boys in the town and he certainly wasn't the best behaved. He envied the Giant, both for his size and his badness. When you are as large as a giant there are a great many extra ways of being bad and the Giant tried most of them. He lived over the hill behind the town, but sometimes he crossed the field where the saw-mill was and if the smoke was coming out of the tall chimney he leaned over and blew down it so that the men who were working in the mill coughed and spluttered. Sometimes in the early morning he reached a finger to the school house bell hanging high against the roof, and all the children, halfway through their breakfasts, gulped and gobbled and raced into school half an hour early. Once when Tom was sailing his boats in the river the Giant decided it was a good day to take a swim farther upstream, and he enjoyed it so much that he lay on his back, kicking and splashing. Water rose up round him in fountains and then poured downstream in great waves, so that Tom's boats were swamped, and those that didn't sink were tossed against the bank with their rigging tangled and the thin stick masts smashed into pieces. That was bad enough, but a week later while Tom was out on the hill flying his new kite the Giant walked by, tangling the string of the kite in his bootlaces so that the kite came down in the middle of a gorse bush, all torn and broken.

Tom picked up the bits and carried them home. 'I'll get even with that Giant, see if I don't,' he growled all the way down the hill, and the wind heard him and laughed: 'Get even with the Giant! I'd like to see you manage it! What could you do, a boy your size, a button of a boy, a pinhole person, what could you do to beat a Giant as big and as bad as that Giant is?'

'You wait and see,' Tom promised, 'just you wait! I may not be big but I know how to be bad!'

But what could he do? Perhaps the wind had been right. Tom thought about it for a week. One day when school was over he went across the hill into the valley where the Giant lived. He had never been there before. It was a bare, grey, lonely place, rocks, little grass, and one tall leafless tree at the dark entrance where the Giant made his home.

Tom decided to hide behind a rock and wait for the Giant. The sun had gone down, the shadows were long and blue and there was a cool moon in the sky when the Giant came home. He tramped up the valley whistling a tune to himself, and the noise he made was as loud as the town's flute band when they were out on parade. When he reached the mouth of the cave the Giant kicked off his boots, one first and then the other, hung his shabby hat on the top of the tree and went into the cave for his supper and his bed.

Tom tiptoed out from behind the rock. He stared up at the Giant's hat. It was the size of a bath. Even if he did get up to the top of the tree there would be no chance of shifting it. He leaned over the edge of one of the boots. 'He wouldn't go far without these,' he decided, and he put one of the laces over his shoulder and bent his back and heaved. But it was no use, the Giant's boot was so heavy that Tom couldn't budge it even an inch.

'No use,' teased the wind, 'no use at all. What can you do, a feather-boned boy the size of you?'

But Tom had an idea. Glue was what he needed and his father was a carpenter so he knew where glue could be found. The following evening after it was dark Tom carried a pot of glue into the Giant's valley. The boots were there. Tom emptied half of the pot of glue into one boot and half into the other and went off home to his bed.

Next morning what a commotion from

the other side of the hill, what a stamping and a thumping, what a roaring and a bellowing! It went on all day, so that no one in the town heard the church clock chiming or the school bell ringing, and not a single hen in any hen-house laid a single egg. It was late in the evening and the townspeople were almost distracted when they heard first one tremendous crash and then another, then a sigh like a steam engine blowing off steam, and after that silence. 'I wonder what all that was about,' they said to each other as they collected the babies and put them to bed. Tom smiled. He knew.

That night the wind whistled down his bedroom chimney: 'Bully for you, Tom, bully for you, bully for yoo-oo-ou!' 'I told you, didn't I?' Tom said, and he put his head below the blankets and went to sleep.

For several weeks no one heard much of the giant. 'He's lying low,' they said to each other. 'He's run out of ideas,' Tom said to himself. Saturday was the day of the big cricket match, the boys from Tom's town were playing the boys from a town nearby. It was always a very important day, and specially important this year for Tom because he had been chosen to play in the team. He ached for the feeling of the bat in his hands. This would be a day for lifting the ball high into the sky. What a match this was going to be! The teams with their supporters trooped up to the cricket pitch.

But the Giant had got there first. There he was, stretched out at his ease from one side of the pitch to the other. That was how they found him, very peaceful and comfortable, his hands clasped behind his head, one foot across the other. His eyes were closed, he was fast asleep!

They shouted and they yelled and the Giant woke up but didn't move. They tried arguing. The Headmaster of the school appealed to the Giant's better feelings. 'Better feelings? Never heard of them,' the Giant said and plucked up a cricket stump to use as a tooth-pick. The boldest of the boys poked and prodded, but it was no use. How could anyone play cricket with a giant lying in the way? And to make it worse the Giant had fallen asleep again.

'Now what'll you do? Now what'll you-oo-oo-ou do-oo-oo?' whistled the wind in Tom's ears. And Tom knew exactly what to do. He passed the word around and in no time at all the fire brigade arrived with their hoses, and it wasn't long before a drenched and dripping Giant, a gasping, soaked, indignant Giant was on his feet and off up the hill with the water running down his neck and out of his ears.

So the match was played and Tom was the hero of the day, both for the runs he scored and for the way he had got the better of the Giant. 'Beautiful,' the wind said that evening, ruffling his bedroom curtains, 'beau-eau-eau-tiful!'

But the Giant caught a cold from his wetting and he wasn't the only one to suffer from it; all the next week the town was shaken by his enormous sneezes, windows rattled, doors came unlatched, ornaments fell off the mantelpieces, babies woke and cried, there was no peace at all. 'He does it out of badness, that's what it is!' people said as another tremendous sneeze rocked the tea in their teacups and made the bread and butter slide off the plates, 'just out of badness, that's all.'

At the end of a week the sneezing stopped. 'The Giant's cold is better,' they said to each other. No sound at all came from the Giant's valley. This was very odd. 'Has he gone away?' they asked, 'he's never been as quiet as this.' 'Perhaps he's sorry,' someone suggested, but nobody really believed that. And in any case they had other things to think about. The new Town Hall was finished at last, the handsome building that had been rising slowly at the head of the street was completed, all but the weathercock which was to sit on the top of the little spire on the roof. The Mayor had invited the mayors and their ladies and the important people from towns and villages many miles round to come on Saturday for a celebration. What a day it was to be – bands, flags, fine clothes, dancing in the streets. No wonder they forgot about the Giant.

But they didn't forget about him for long because two things happened. Mr Clamber the steeplejack hurt his leg and had to stay in bed, and the builders of the Town Hall reported that the crane which was to hoist the handsome gilt weathercock to its proud place on the top of the spire had broken and there was no chance of repairing it in time. What could be done?

Nobody knew who it was who first whispered 'The Giant could help!' Somebody whispered it and somebody else heard them and soon the whisper was so loud that everybody knew about it. 'The Giant might help if he was asked. Someone will have to ask him!'

Who? Who could ask the Giant? The Mayor and two of his Aldermen went over into the Giant's valley on Friday evening, looking very serious and important. 'He won't come,' Tom said, 'catch him coming! Catch him obliging anyone!'

But to the surprise of everyone the Mayor returned to say that the Giant had agreed to come that very evening. So the policeman moved the crowds to the side of the street and cleared away some of the parked cars so that the Giant could walk without his great boots knocking into them. 'Here he comes!' the onlookers said, and at last there was the Giant himself, huge and slow, and a little shy because people were very glad to see him.

He picked up the weathercock between his finger and thumb. 'Nice bit of work here,' he said. They explained to him how it was to be bolted into its place at the top of the spire. They handed him the nuts which looked like grains of sand in his enormous palm.

'No good,' the Giant said, 'they're too small, and my fingers are too big. I couldn't work with those, not if I tried for a year I couldn't.' Then his eyes travelled over the crowd and lit on Tom. 'But this young fellow could,' he said, 'he has the right size of hands for the job.' And before he knew just what was happening Tom had the nuts thrust into one hand and a spanner placed in the other, he felt the great finger and thumb of the Giant nip him round his middle, and up he rose into the sky!

How odd it was up there, high above the roofs, with all those faces staring at him from under his feet and the Giant's warm hand tight round him! With his other hand the Giant had placed the golden bird in its position. 'Now young fellow!' the Giant said as he swung Tom over beside the weathercock. In no time at all Tom's hands had put the nuts on and tightened them.

What was that curious noise coming up from the sea of pink faces? Cheering, that was what it was, they were cheering! The cheers grew louder and louder still as the Giant lowered Tom and set him on the ground again. How splendid the weather-cock looked up there in the evening sky with the last of the evening sunlight brightening its feathers. What a grand day they would have tomorrow, after all. What a good-hearted fellow the Giant was, how clever Tom had been.

'Did you hear that?' teased the wind in Tom's ear, 'cheering for you! For you and the Giant!' but the cheering was so loud that Tom took no notice at all.

Acknowledgements

The editor and publishers gratefully acknowledge the following, for permission to reproduce copyright material in this anthology.

'A Necklace of Raindrops' by Joan Aiken from *A Necklace of Raindrops and Other Stories* published by Puffin Books 1975, copyright © Joan Aiken Enterprises Ltd, 1975, reprinted by permission of the author c/o A M Heath & Company Ltd; 'Secrets' by Anita Desai from *Guardian Angels* edited by Stephanie Nettell published by Puffin Books 1988, copyright © Anita Desai, 1988, reprinted by permission of the author c/o Rogers, Coleridge & White Ltd, London; 'Tsipporah' by Adèle Geras from *The Kingfisher Book of Scary Stories* compiled by Chris Powling published by Kingfisher Books 1994, copyright © Adèle Geras, 1994, reprinted by permission of the author; 'Once There Were No Pandas' by Margaret Greaves published by Methuen Children's Books 1985, copyright © The Literary Estate of Margaret Greaves, 1985, reprinted by permission of Marilyn Malin Consultancy and Representation; 'Mighty Mountain and Three Strong Women' by Irene Hedlund, originally published by Fremad, Copenhagen 1982, English version published by A & C Black (Publishers) Limited 1984, copyright © Irene Hedlund, 1982, reprinted by permission of A & C Black (Publishers) Limited; 'A Fish of the World' by Terry Jones from *Fairy Tales* published by Pavilion Books 1981, copyright © Terry Jones, 1981, reprinted by permission of Pavilion Books; 'The Girl Who Stayed for Half a Week' by

ACKNOWLEDGEMENTS

Gene Kemp from *Roundabout* published by Faber and Faber Ltd 1993, copyright © Gene Kemp, 1993, reprinted by permission of Faber and Faber Ltd; 'The Palace of Boundless Gold' from *In the Court of the Jade Emperor: Stories from Old China* by Rosalind Kerven published by Cambridge University Press 1993, copyright © Cambridge University Press, 1993; reprinted by permission of the author and Cambridge University Press; 'King Midas' retold by Geraldine McCaughrean from *The Orchard Book of Greek Myths* published by Orchard Books 1992, copyright © Geraldine McCaughrean, 1992, reprinted by permission of Orchard Books, a division of the Watts Publishing Group; 'The Gigantic Badness' by Janet McNeill from *Bad Boys* edited by Eileen Colwell published by Puffin Books 1972, copyright © David Alexander, 1970, reprinted by permission of A P Watt Ltd on behalf of David Alexander; 'A Picnic with the Aunts' by Ursula Moray Williams from *Bad Boys* edited by Eileen Colwell published by Puffin Books 1972, copyright © Ursula Moray Williams, 1972, reprinted by permission of Curtis Brown Ltd, London on behalf of Ursula Moray Williams; 'Dog, Cat and Monkey' from *South, North, East and West: The Oxfam Book of Children's Stories* edited by Michael Rosen published by Walker Books Ltd 1992, edited copyright © Michael Rosen, 1992, copyright © Oxfam Activities, 1992, reprinted by permission of Walker Books Ltd, London.

Choosing a brilliant book
can be a tricky business...
but not any more

www.puffin.co.uk

The best selection of books at your fingertips

So get clicking!

Searching the site is easy – you'll find
what you're looking for at the click of a mouse,
from great authors to brilliant books and more!

Everyone's got different taste . . .

I like stories that make me laugh

Animal stories are definitely my favourite

I'd say fantasy is the best

I like a bit of romance

It's got to be adventure for me

I really love poetry

I like a good mystery

Whatever you're into, we've got it covered . . .

www.puffin.co.uk

hotnews@puffin

Hot off the press!

You'll find all the latest exclusive Puffin news here

Where's it happening?

Check out our author tours and events programme

Best-sellers

What's hot and what's not? Find out in our charts

E-mail updates

Sign up to receive all the latest news
straight to your e-mail box

Links to the coolest sites

Get connected to all the best author web sites

Book of the Month

Check out our recommended reads

www.puffin.co.uk

Choosing a brilliant book
can be a tricky business...
but not any more

www.puffin.co.uk

The best selection of books at your fingertips

So get clicking!

Searching the site is easy – you'll find
what you're looking for at the click of a mouse,
from great authors to brilliant books and more!

Read more in Puffin

For complete information about books available from Puffin – and Penguin – and how to order them, contact us at the appropriate address below. Please note that for copyright reasons the selection of books varies from country to country.

www.puffin.co.uk

In the United Kingdom: Please write to Dept EP, Penguin Books Ltd,
Bath Road, Harmondsworth, West Drayton, Middlesex UB7 0DA

In the United States: Please write to Penguin Putnam Inc., P.O. Box 12289,
Dept B, Newark, New Jersey 07101–5289 or call 1–800–788–6262

In Canada: Please write to Penguin Books Canada Ltd,
10 Alcorn Avenue, Suite 300, Toronto, Ontario M4V 3B2

In Australia: Please write to Penguin Books Australia Ltd,
P.O. Box 257, Ringwood, Victoria 3134

In New Zealand: Please write to Penguin Books (NZ) Ltd,
Private Bag 102902, North Shore Mail Centre, Auckland 10

In India: Please write to Penguin Books India Pvt Ltd,
11 Panscheel Shopping Centre, Panscheel Park, New Delhi 110 017

In the Netherlands: Please write to Penguin Books Netherlands bv,
Postbus 3507, NL–1001 AH Amsterdam

In Germany: Please write to Penguin Books Deutschland GmbH,
Metzlerstrasse 26, 60594 Frankfurt am Main

In Spain: Please write to Penguin Books S. A., Bravo Murillo 19,
1° B, 28015 Madrid

In Italy: Please write to Penguin Italia s.r.l.,
Via Felice Casati 20, I–20124 Milano

In France: Please write to Penguin France S. A.,
17 rue Lejeune, F–31000 Toulouse

In Japan: Please write to Penguin Books Japan, Ishikiribashi Building,
2–5–4, Suido, Bunkyo-ku, Tokyo 112

In South Africa: Please write to Longman Penguin Southern Africa (Pty) Ltd,
Private Bag X08, Bertsham 2013